Eye of the Storm:
The First Token

Book 1
Time Game Series

D. A. Featherling

TIMEGAME

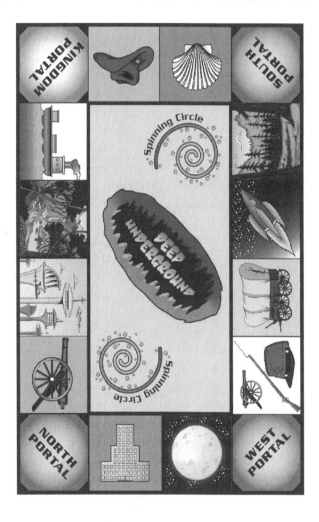

DEDICATION

To the brave men and women
who sailed the Great Lakes,
and to the memory of
those who perished there.

IN MEMORIAM

The Crew of the *L. R. Doty*

Captain Christopher Smith *of Port Huron, MI*
Henry Sharp, *First Mate of Detroit*
W. J. Bossie, Second Mate of Detroit
Thomas Abernathie, *Engineer of Port Huron, MI*
C. W. Odette, *Second Engineer*
George Wadkin, *Oiler*
L. Goss, *Steward of Bay City, MI*
W. J. Scott, *Cook*
Charles Bornie, *Watchman*
Peter G. Peterson, *Wheelsman*
Albert Nelson, *Assistant Wheelsman*
Joseph Fitzsimmons, *Fireman*
J. Howe, *Deckhand*
F. Parmuth, *Deckhand*
C. Curtis, *Deckhand*
William Ebert, *Deckhand*
Pat Ryan, *Deckhand*
Dewey and Watson, *The ship's two cats*

The Crew of the Olive Jeanette

Captain David B. Cadotte
Hiram Combs, *Mate*
Herbert Mills, *Seaman*
James Meisener, *Seaman*
John McQuarry, *Seaman*
William McCormick, *Seaman*
Miss Frances Browne, *Cook*

ACKNOWLEDGMENTS

A number of people helped make this fictional tale more historically accurate.

Special thanks to those who work to discover and preserve marine underwater archeological sites for their contributions to Great Lakes marine history.

Thanks to Jonathon Featherling for technical assistance and comments, to beta readers, Peggy Caravantes, Jonathon Featherling, and Linda Farmer Harris.

A 'thank you' to my critique group for their suggestions. A special thanks to Jonathon and Joseph Featherling for helpful discussions.

Thanks to board illustrator Dave Allred (davedesigns70@gmail.com)

And as always, my greatest thanks and appreciation to my Lord, Jesus Christ, for letting me be an author.

CHAPTER 1

"Boo!"

"Aghhh!"

"Gotcha." Marcus Willoughby gave a gleeful laugh at the expression on his twin's face as he jumped from behind the rickety dresser and grabbed her shoulders.

Samantha slapped at him. "Marko, that's not funny."

"Yeah, it was." Marcus dodged the blow and moved backwards. "Betcha thought I was a ghost." He waved a hand at the huge attic room where they stood. "This place is so gloomy; it ought to have a ghost or two."

His sister looked around. "It's pretty weird, all right, but you know there aren't any such things as ghosts."

He shrugged. "If there were, they'd be here. C'mon, Sami. Let's explore. Mom and Dad are busy downstairs, so we've got a little time before they're ready to leave."

He strode to the center of the large room. It had obviously been used as storage for many years. Furniture stood around the walls, most of it in disrepair. Sofas with broken springs slumped against dressers and bureaus with handle-less drawers. Chest and trunks leaned in crazy confusion against each other.

"This place could be a warehouse." He made a slow pivot as he continued his assessment. "I don't know if there's anything valuable in here or if it's all junk."

Samantha nodded and walked to a cobweb-covered dresser shoved against one wall. She swiped her hand across it, looked in disgust at the gray layer of dust now smeared on her fingers. "Gross. You'd think Mom's Great-Uncle Henry would have kept the place a little cleaner."

Marcus turned toward a large trunk set against the opposite wall. "From what Mom said about him, I don't think he was much into cleaning. He was some kind of inventor or something…made all kinds of crazy stuff nobody could use."

His sister smirked. "Sounds like somebody else in the family."

"Hey. I think of neat stuff to do. You have to admit some of my ideas are really cool."

"Sure. Like the robot you tried to design to clean your room? That went well."

Marcus grinned. "Okay. Maybe it didn't work quite right, but it got me a prize in the science competition at school."

"Honestly, Marko." Sami fisted her hands on her hips. "Sometimes I wonder if you're twelve years old or a two-year-old in boy clothes."

He tugged at the trunk until it sat in the center of the room. "Hmmph. I'm older than you."

"Yeah, by two minutes. We're twins, remember? We were born at almost the same time."

"Big deal. Who cares?" Marcus made a face at her.

Samantha turned away and wandered toward another dust-covered piece of furniture. "I wonder if there's anything in these drawers." She reached for the nearest handle.

"Dunno. I'm trying to get this trunk open. Maybe Great-Uncle Henry left a treasure in it."

"I doubt it. Mom said he didn't have much money while he was alive since most of his inventions didn't work. Like someone else's...."

"We've already had that conversation." Marcus ignored his sister's snort and concentrated on prying open the trunk lid.

As it gave way, his mother's voice came from downstairs. "Guys, let's go! Time to head home!"

"Awwwww!" Sami pushed the drawer shut. "We just got here!"

"You heard me." Their mother's voice increased a couple of degrees. "Come on. It'll be lunch time soon."

Marcus cupped his hands around his mouth. "Can we have something to take with us?"

"If it's small, I guess so. But hurry. We need to leave."

Marcus threw open the lid of the trunk. Still more dust covered the surface of the objects inside. "Phew." He sneezed as a cloud of particles invaded his nose.

"Kids." The warning this time in his mother's tone was unmistakable.

"Come on, Marko." Samantha headed for the

staircase. "There's probably nothing in the old trunk worth having anyway."

Marcus leaned over and picked up the top item. A shabby old box. He lifted it and blew off the dust. Another sneeze sprayed the lid. He noticed Samantha had already disappeared down the stairs.

"Marcus."

The sound of his mother's voice moved Marcus forward.

"Coming." He took the stairs two at a time, juggling the cardboard box as he went. He gave a doubtful glance at it. He could only hope there was either something valuable, or at least interesting, inside. He'd have to wait until he got home to find out.

CHAPTER 2

"What're you doing?" Samantha interrupted Marcus's concentration.

"Finding out what's in here."

"What is it?"

"There's a game board with pictures and stuff on it." He pointed toward a small stack of tokens. "These were on top when I opened the lid."

Each token had a little picture stamped on it. So far he'd found one with the outline of a ship, another with some type of building, and a third showing a round disc that looked like the moon or a planet. The others remained face down.

He shrugged. "I have *no* clue what these things are or what they're for."

"Let me have the ship one," said Samantha. "Where's the board? I'll put the token in the right place." She leaned over, balanced against his shoulder, picked up the token and set it down.

A moment later she let out a faint cry.

"What's wrong?" Marcus jerked his gaze away from studying the board and looked at his sister. Her entire body shimmered.

"What are you doing?" Marcus was half-angry, half-frightened. "Why are you shimmering?"

"I don't know, but I want it to stop! It's scary." She pulled her hand away from the board. The shimmer disappeared.

Marcus stared at her. "Do that again."

She shook her head. "No way. It was too weird. Felt like…like I was starting to come apart."

"How do you mean come apart?"

Samantha glared at him. "Didn't you see what happened? Something odd is going on here. I think you need to trash the silly game and forget about it."

"No, Sami. We need to check it out. Maybe Great-Uncle Henry wasn't such a failure as an inventor after all. Who knows what might be going on with the game?"

"You don't know if he invented it or not. Maybe he bought it somewhere. Maybe it's been in the attic too long and picked up some kind of electrical charge and it shocked me a little."

"Did you feel anything like electricity when the shimmer started?"

"No-o-o-o, but it could have been too slight to notice." Samantha backed away from where Marcus sat. She rubbed the hand that had touched the token. "It was weird."

"Look." He made himself sound patient. "I know you're the brains in the family. Miss Do-Everything-Right. But I want to know what happened when you touched the board. Or maybe it was the token."

Samantha edged closer, peeked over his shoulder again without getting too close. "Don't pick up the tokens. Let's check out the board first. Maybe it'll tell us something."

"What fun is that?"

"Marko, I'm serious. If the game is some invention of Great-Uncle Henry's it could be dangerous. Maybe we should tell Mom and Dad and let them decide what to do with it."

"No. It's my game. Mom said I could have something and I chose this. If you don't want to know what's going on, fine. I'll figure it out by myself." He turned away from her. "I never thought you were a fraidy-cat."

"I'm not afraid."

"Are too."

"Am not. I'm…cautious."

"Yeah, right."

"Look." Samantha moved closer. "Let's try to analyze it. Maybe we can see what's going on without harming ourselves. We have to be careful."

"So what do you suggest we do, Miss Scientific Experimenter?"

She ignored him and leaned forward to peer inside the box. "Let's read the directions and see what they say about how to play the game. Where are they?"

"There aren't any."

"No directions? What kind of a game doesn't have directions?"

"This kind, I guess." Marcus propped his chin on his hand. "It is kind of odd, though, isn't it?"

"Very."

"I wonder if Great-Uncle Henry actually invented the game?"

Marcus's question rang loud in the room.

Silence fell as they studied the box sitting on the floor.

Finally, Marcus heaved a sigh and reached for the game board.

"Stop, Marko. Don't touch it."

"Back off, Sami. I can't tell anything about the board if I can't see it clearly. The illustrations and lettering are so faint it's hard to make out exactly what's on it."

Before she could react, Marcus grabbed the board and held it toward the window. He paused for a moment, waiting to see what would happen.

Nothing did.

"There." He let himself sound triumphant. "See, nothing. Nada. It must have been our imagination."

"It wasn't imagination."

"Well, I'm holding the board and nothing has happened to me, has it?"

"No."

"Then…it must have been our imagination."

"Maybe." Samantha turned and walked to the other side of the room. "But to be safe, I'm standing over here while you look at the thing. Tell me what you see."

"Oh, sure. Let me be in danger while you watch."

"Thought you said nothing happened."

"Nothing did. Doesn't mean it couldn't." Marcus held the board first one way, then another, trying to make out the specifics of the game.

He brushed one hand over the board in a dusting motion, even though he knew it had been wiped off right after he got it out of the box.

"Wha...."

"What do you mean 'what'?" Samantha took a step toward her brother, then froze. "What do you see, Marko?"

"I...I can't tell exactly. It seemed when I brushed off the board, everything on it got brighter."

"Maybe it has a light in it somewhere and you triggered it."

"I don't think so." Marcus tilted the board toward the window again where sunlight streamed in. "Would you look at that."

CHAPTER 3

"What do you see?" Samantha took a couple more steps forward before she stopped. "Tell me what's going on, Marko."

"Come on over here and look for yourself." Marcus gestured at her impatiently. "It's not going to bite you."

Samantha edged toward him, one cautious step at a time until she reached his side. "Let me see."

"Here." Marcus held the board toward her. "Aren't things much brighter?"

She made a careful survey. "Maybe. Or maybe you held it where the light wasn't hitting it correctly."

"I did, too. I tell you, Sami, it got brighter when I did this." Marcus passed his hand over the board again.

Two gasps split the air at almost the same moment.

"Look, it got even brighter." Samantha's voice held a note of awe and a healthier note of fear. "Put it away. The thing is haunted."

"Thought you said there wasn't any such thing as a ghost." Marcus teased her.

"There isn't...but...."

"I think dear old Great-Uncle Henry must have

been on to something, Sami. We need to know what's involved in the game and why it acts the way it does. Are you with me or not?"

Samantha stood for a moment, indecision showing in every line of her body. She finally gave a slow nod. "Okay. But only in the name of science and knowledge."

"Oh, brother. Why don't you admit you're curious, too, and let's get on with it?"

"Okay. Okay. I'm curious. Let's figure the thing out. But...we do it carefully, deal?"

"Deal." Marcus placed the board back on the floor, scooted it closer to the window where the light would hit it directly. "You sit over there. I'll stay on this side. Let's try to read what the words on it say and decipher the pictures. I'll do this half of the board and you do the side facing you."

"Right." Samantha's tone was brisk. She did love to solve problems. "I'll go first."

Marcus cleared his throat. "Who's the oldest?"

"Fine. Go first."

He studied his half of the board. "I wonder." He passed his hand over the board another time and watched – half in awe, half in expectation – as the board once again further cleared the lines and words it contained.

"Let's give it a couple more swipes, Sami, and get it as clear as we can."

They took turns brushing their hands across the board.

"That's three times," said Samantha. "It didn't get any brighter or clearer the third time."

"Yeah. Guess we've got it at maximum power."

"It's not a spaceship, Marko. We're not blasting off."

"We might be. It's the strangest thing I've ever seen. I wonder, though, why did you get all shimmery when you touched it before but you haven't since we've been swiping at the board?"

"Maybe because we weren't touching the token. The token could be the key."

Marcus reached for the stack of tokens. "Let's find out."

"No. Don't." Samantha scrambled backward.

He stirred the tokens with the tip of his finger. "There. Did I shimmer?"

Samantha watched as he moved the tokens around again. "No." She resumed her place by the board. "Do you suppose…it was me?"

"What do you mean?"

"I mean, did I make it happen?"

"Only one way to find out." Marcus shoved the stack of tokens toward her. "Touch one and see what happens."

Samantha reached out a tentative finger, but stopped short of making contact. "Marko, I'm afraid. What if I go all shimmery again?"

"Then take your finger off the token, silly."

She sat there, not moving. "Maybe…maybe we should pray or something."

"You're kidding, right?"

Samantha shook her head.

He sat for a minute. Slowly his expression went from scornful to thoughtful. "Actually, it's a good idea. If we're on the edge of a discovery...or an adventure...we sure want God to be there with us."

"He would be anyway," said Samantha. "But it's better if we actually invite Him to be in on this."

"Right." Marcus bowed his head. "I'll pray."

Samantha bowed her head as well. "Go on. You're the oldest."

He looked at her, then bowed his head again. "Dear God. We don't know what's going on with the board and these tokens, but we ask You to keep us safe and be with us as we explore the possibilities."

"And, be with us if anything bad happens and rescue us." Samantha's words followed on top of Marcus's.

"Amen." They chorused the word together.

"That's better." Samantha smiled and reached for the nearest token. Gripping her bottom lip between her teeth, she touched the ship token she'd held earlier. It slid along the floor a few millimeters.

"Feel anything?" Marcus's gaze flitted from her hand to her face and back to her hand.

"No, nothing." Samantha's relief was obvious. She shoved at the little pile of tokens. "Guess it's not the tokens or me."

"Hmmm." Marcus concentrated his gaze on the tokens. He looked from them to the board and back again.

"Move those tokens out of the way, Sami. Let's focus on the board and see what's on it now the pictures and words are clearer."

"Okay." Samantha scooted the tokens to one side.

They leaned forward, staring hard at the board.

"Tell me about the side nearest you," said Marcus. "Then I'll describe mine. Tell me what you see."

"Okay."

They both looked at their sides of the board.

Samantha broke the silence with a huge sigh. "All right. Here's what I see."

Marcus shifted his attention to her side of the board.

Samantha pointed to the corner to her left. "It says 'Kingdom Portal.' The corner to my right is labeled 'North Portal.'"

"Wow. Portals. Sounds like time travel stuff. Remember the movie we saw where portals were doorways into strange places and different times?" Awe was in Marcus's voice. "Wait a minute. Let me tell you about my side of the board. My two corners say 'West Portal' on the left corner and 'South Portal on the right.'"

"That covers all the directions except the East." Samantha sat for a moment. "Wonder why there's not one labeled 'East Portal.'"

Marcus stared at the board, thinking hard. "Dunno. But let's worry about it later and check the rest of the board. I've also got three squares between my two portals."

Samantha interrupted him. "And there are three other squares across from those between the Kingdom Portal and the North Portal."

"Uh huh."

Samantha sounded less afraid. "And in the middle there are three more on each side between portals."

"Yep. And...." Marcus pointed, "every square has

a picture on it. There's a ship. It's the same one on the token."

Samantha gestured. "And there's a building."

"Yeah, there was one of those on a token, too." Marcus gave a little bounce. "Look, over here next to the ship square is the planet or moon or whatever it is. I'll bet each square has a matching token."

"But there are more squares than there are tokens." Samantha gestured toward the board. "Counting the squares all the way around the board, there should be twelve tokens. There aren't that many." She poked at the pile of tokens.

"Maybe there are more inside." Marcus reached for the box and shook it. A rattle sounded. He removed the cardboard panel from inside the box. "Ha. Here's more stuff."

Tilting the box upside down, he poured a stream of objects on the floor.

CHAPTER 4

"Don't let them get away."

They both scrambled, trapping tokens and other items from going under the furniture. When they had gathered everything, they resumed their places. Shoving the board aside, Marcus and Samantha deposited their findings on the floor.

Samantha pointed to several brightly colored objects. "What in the world are those?"

Marcus selected a red one. "It's a red stone of some kind. Very smooth surface." He poked around in the pile. "Here's a green one, and a blue, and a yellow."

"Wonder what part those have in the game?" Samantha queried in an analytical tone. "Why couldn't Great-Uncle Henry have included some instructions for the game? It's almost worthless without them."

"Don't be in such a hurry." Marcus made a shooing motion in her direction. "Let's finish checking out what we've got here." He poked at a red die with white markings. "At least it uses dice." He stirred the pile with his forefinger. "Well, one die anyway."

"Fine." Samantha pouted, but pulled the board

back in front of them. "Here. We need to finish checking the squares and things and try to figure out what they mean."

The two concentrated on the board.

Finally, Marcus, who'd been fingering the red stone, switched it to his left hand and gestured at the two circles drawn in opposite interior corners labeled 'Spinning Circles.' "What do you think those mean?"

"Dunno. Doesn't make any sense to me." Samantha dismissed his comment and did her own pointing. "Here's something in between them marked 'Deep Underground.' Wonder what that's about?"

"This is getting harder and harder." Marcus pounded his fist on the floor. "I may just trash this thing and forget it."

"No. Wait. Let's take some more time to experiment."

"You experiment." Marcus stood, slid one hand into the pocket of his shorts. "I need a snack." He headed for the door, gave a casual wave to his sister who was studying the puzzle lying on the floor in front of her.

Samantha didn't respond.

# # # #

Half an hour later, Marcus emitted a loud belch as he re-entered the room.

Samantha frowned at him. "That's disgusting."

Marcus grinned. "You're jealous because you can't do it."

"As if I'd want to."

He walked over to where she sat on the floor. "You figured the thing out yet?"

"No. I'm about ready to agree with you. It probably needs to hit the trash."

"Fine by me." Marcus turned and started to walk away. Before he reached the door, he stopped. "Wait a minute. We need to conduct an experiment first."

"An experiment? What kind of experiment?"

"How about if we try to play the game?"

"How could we do that?"

Marcus sat down opposite her. He picked up a couple of the tokens. "Let's put the tokens on the matching squares on the board. Maybe something will happen and we can decide what to do next."

Samantha shrugged. "Okay, but I don't think it's going to help."

They placed tokens on the appropriate squares. When they finished, only the die and the little pile of colored stones were left.

"Where do you suppose those go?" Samantha gestured toward them.

"No idea. Leave them for now."

The two studied the board in silence.

"Any ideas?" Marcus finally broke their concentration.

"Nope. Well, maybe one." Samantha poked at the token containing the picture of the ship. "Why don't we try moving the tokens around one at a time? We can put them on the different drawings on the board and see what takes place."

"That's an idea. You're touching the ship. Go ahead. Push it somewhere else."

Samantha placed the tip of her finger on the token, shoved it toward the area marked 'Deep Underground.'

Nothing.

She moved it to one of the Spinning Circles, then the other. Again, nothing.

Samantha pushed the token to each of the portals, pausing for a moment on each one. Still nothing.

"That was a waste of time." Marcus knew he sounded accusing.

"Not my fault," said Samantha. "Here. You try it. Maybe it'll do something for you." She shoved the ship token toward Marcus.

He reached forward and placed his fingertip on top of hers.

"Gotcha." He pressed down on her finger, moved the token toward one of the circles. "Let's see if we can spin."

"Don't be an idiot, Marko." Samantha tried to pull her hand away from her brother's touch as he moved the token onto the nearest spinning circle. "Let me go."

"Whoa...." Marcus swallowed. Dizziness and a little nausea hit him. He stared at his twin. What was wrong? She appeared fuzzy, began to grow dim. "Sami...."

From a long way away he heard her. "Marko...."

CHAPTER 5

Marcus's head throbbed. He tried to swallow the dryness from his mouth. It didn't help much. What was wrong with him? He felt terrible. Little bumps pressed along his spine as he lay on something that shifted every few minutes. He could also detect a motion like floating in a swimming pool on an inner tube. Nausea threatened.

He groaned.

"Marko?"

"Sami? Where are you? It's dark. I can't see anything."

"Over here."

Marcus frowned. "I don't know where 'here' is. Can you see anything?"

"No. Oh, Marcus, I think I'm going to be sick."

"Don't you dare." He swallowed his own queasiness again. "Reach out your hands to your sides one at a time and see if we can touch each other."

He focused on straightening his left arm and moving it in a slow arc. "Anything?"

"No." Samantha shook her head. "You?"

"No. Try with the other arm." Marcus switched to moving his right arm. Halfway through the movement, he touched something. He grasped for the solid object. "Is that you?"

His sister clutched his hand. "Oh, Marko. Thank goodness." She sounded near tears.

"Easy, Sami. I've got you."

They lay there, fingers intertwined.

Marcus turned his head from side to side on the uncomfortable small lumps. A musty odor filled his nostrils.

"Sami, do you smell anything?"

"Yeah. Reminds me of old vegetables."

Marcus heart thumped, his throat parched again. Were they in a garbage dump?

"Smells dusty to me," he said. "More like something dried up."

"I'm lying on little lumps, Marko. And they're shifting under me."

Marcus didn't mention his garbage dump theory. No point in panicking his sister. He moved his free hand and dug it into the lumps. His fingers traced the outline of what felt like a good-sized seed. Seemed almost tooth-shaped.

"Sami, use your other hand and feel the lumps one at a time. What do you think it is?" He wouldn't have admitted it, but he didn't intend to let go of his sister's hand. In the darkness it was his only connection with reality. Not that he was afraid. Well, maybe a little bit.

He fingered the object he held. "You know, it reminds me of a dried kernel of corn. Remember how those felt the time we visited the farmer's market and somebody had shucked a cob of corn onto the ground? These are about the same size. Feel it."

"Let me try." Silence for a moment, then Samantha's excitement came through loud and clear. "It *is* corn, Marko. We're lying on a huge pile of corn kernels."

"Why would we be doing that?"

"I don't know. Can you sit up?"

Marcus grasped Sami's hand tighter. "Don't let go. We don't want to lose each other in here. Wherever we are."

"Right. I'll stay still. You try to sit up, okay?"

He rolled halfway toward the sound of Samantha's voice. "Ouch. This is the lumpiest bed I've ever been on." He struggled to move. The corn shifted around him. As he tensed his legs to try to sit up, more kernels shifted. His legs sank into them. "Whoa."

"What's wrong?" Panic drenched Samantha's response. "What happened?"

He stilled. "Moving isn't such a good idea." He swallowed hard. "When I try to sit up, the kernels cover my legs and I sink. I'm afraid if I move too much the corn will bury me."

"Then don't move, Marko." Samantha's clutch on his hand tightened. "We'd better stay still. I wonder where we are."

"It must have been that dumb game. What was Great-Uncle Henry thinking? He designed something dangerous. I wish I'd never seen the thing."

"You didn't know." Samantha comforted him. "We were trying out the board. And now we're...where?"

"Dunno." Marcus lay still, felt more of the underlying swaying motion. Each time a sway occurred, the corn shifted around him. If the movement continued would it eventually bury them? He had to be brave, though. He needed to take care of his sister, even though he knew she'd say she could take care of herself. "Let's try moving our heads a little to each side, Sami, and see if we can see anything."

"Right."

Marcus gently rolled his head to the right toward where Samantha lay. He couldn't see a thing, not even a vague outline of his sister. Continuing in a slow motion, he looked to his left side. Nothing, although there did seem to be a little lightening of the darkness in that direction.

He stared harder. What was that?

Two spots of red showed in his vision. He blinked once...twice. Now he was seeing things.

No. He did see something...red spots.

"Sami." He tried to keep his tone calm and unworried. "Turn your head to the left toward me and tell me what you see."

"Okay."

It was quiet for a moment before Samantha responded. "Oh, I do see a little something, Marko. Sort of like...like two little red spots."

"Yeah, that's what I thought. What do you suppose they are?"

"Maybe they're lights...LEDs or something."

"Maybe. If they are lights, there must be people around somewhere, don't you think?"

"Of course." Samantha squeezed his hand. "Let's concentrate on the lights and see if we can tell anything else about where we are."

"Okay." Marcus focused on the two red spots. As he gazed, the lights shifted to the right. "Did you see them move?"

"Yeah, I saw." A note of fear colored Samantha's response.

"What do you think it means?"

"Dunno. Either they're moving with the motion we feel…or they're attached to something…alive."

Marcus's throat went drier than a desert. "Alive?" He hated the catch in his voice. "What would be alive here?" He swallowed. "Let's watch a little more."

They both stared in the direction of the two red dots, then stiffened as the lights moved closer.

Samantha's squeak sounded as scared as he did. "They moved again. They're coming toward us, Marko. What are we going to do?"

CHAPTER 6

"Don't move, Sami. If we thrash around, the corn is going to bury us. Let's...let's...pray again."

"Help us, Jesus." Samantha's voice pitched two levels higher than her normal tone.

"Yeah, help us." Marcus echoed her plea.

They lay frozen as they watched the red dots move closer and closer, occasionally veering to one side or the other, but always coming back to focus on them.

Samantha's hand clutched Marcus's even tighter. "Marko...do you think...could it be...a rat?"

His stomach dipped. Rats. He hadn't thought of those. Of course, it made sense. Corn kernels would attract rodents. He gulped.

The dots moved forward, stopped, then resumed their slow approach.

"Listen." Marcus strained his ears. "Do you hear anything?"

"Like what?"

"I don't know. Maybe a low rumble. Kind of like a...cat purring."

"Are you out of your mind? What would a cat be doing in a bunch of corn?"

The dots moved ever closer, the rumble

intensifying as they did.

"Marcus. It *is* a cat." Samantha's hand slipped from his grasp. "Come here, kitty. Nice kitty."

"Don't let go, Sami." Marcus didn't care if his own panic showed. "Grab my hand again."

They fumbled in the darkness until their hands rejoined.

"But it's a cat, Marko. Call it. If there's a cat here, there have to be people somewhere."

If there was a cat, there also might be rats. Probably were.

Marcus kept the thought to himself. He could imagine his sister's reaction if he mentioned the possibility of rodents.

He pretended to sound disgusted. "Oh, great. Now I have to cozy up to a cat."

A hard squeeze of his hand indicated his sister's disapproval.

"Hush. Just call it."

"Fine. Here kitty. Good cat." Marcus wiggled the fingers of his left hand in the animal's general direction.

A minute later, sharp claws grabbed at his fingers.

"Ow. Easy, cat." Marcus felt fur. He stroked the cat and heard the rumbling purr intensify. "If this guy...."

"Or gal...."

"Or gal...belongs to anybody we need to yell, Sami. Maybe they'll hear us and get us out of wherever we are."

"Good idea. On three, let's yell as loud as we can."

"Right. I'll count."

"Boys!" Disgust colored Samantha's tone. "So count."

"One...two...three...."

Both lifted their voices.

Marcus could tell from the echo around them they must be in a large space. Never mind. He continued to make as much noise as he could. Samantha's loud screeching so close to his head made his ears hurt.

A couple of minutes later, a scraping noise came from overhead. A crack of light showed in the darkness.

A man bellowed. "Who's down there?"

They both responded.

"Help." "Get us out of here."

More scraping, more light until a two-foot section of what had been their ceiling moved sideways and revealed a whiskery face. A face wearing an astonished look.

"Kids? What are you doing in the hold? How did you get here?"

Their words blended again as they tried to explain.

"Wait. I can't make out a word you're saying. Hang on. I'll get some help."

He disappeared.

Marcus and Samantha, now able to see each other, smiled.

"We're rescued." Samantha's relief came through clearly.

"Guess our prayers got answered...again."

"They sure did." Samantha withdrew her hand. "Thank goodness."

A short time later, louder scrapes sounded and the hatch slid further aside. A second man's voice drifted downward.

"Now I've seen everything. Who are you kids and why are you stowing away on my vessel?"

Marcus swallowed, tried to respond, but failed.

"Never mind. Let's get you out, then you can answer my questions."

It only took a few minutes for a rope to be lowered to each of the twins. Holding on for dear life, they were pulled up, up, until they were clear of the hold and standing on the deck of the largest ship they'd ever seen. Several men dressed in long-sleeved knit shirts and baggy trousers stood and watched the rescue. Several wore knit caps pulled low over their ears.

A uniformed man confronted them. "Are you two it? Or are there more down there?"

Marcus heard a hint of humor in the question. Relief flooded him as he responded. "Just us."

"And the cat." Samantha chimed in.

"Oh, yeah. There's a cat, too," said Marcus.

"Something you brought aboard? Or one of ours?"

Marcus and Samantha gave each other an astonished glance.

"You have cats on a ship?" Marcus couldn't help being amazed.

"Two. Dewey and Watson," said the officer. "They keep us pest free."

Pests. Rats. Marcus knew the man meant rats. A shudder racked his frame. Thank goodness they didn't have to worry about those any more. He shot a quick glance around. At least not that he could see.

He gave a shaky nod. "Nice."

The man beckoned to the two of them. "Come with me. We need to talk. I have a few questions."

So do I, thought Marcus. *But I'll bet nobody can answer mine. Except maybe for Great-Uncle Henry and I don't think he'll be doing any talking.*

Marcus sniffed as they followed the seaman. Then he took a big lungful of air. Huh! No fishy smell. No salty smell either. Must be a lake. A freshwater lake at that. Seemed odd to see so much water and not have any scent he could identify, except for a faint smell of coal. That must help power the engine.

The twins followed the officer up a staircase and into a corridor. Every man they passed saluted as they went by.

Must be the captain who accompanied them. Marcus grinned at Samantha. She made a face back. Good. Sami was herself again.

A few minutes later they entered what had to be the captain's cabin. Marcus thought the room impressive even though it wasn't very large. A desk filled most of the space. A chair sat behind it and a couple of smaller ones in front. Marcus could see another door behind the desk. Must be the bedroom or whatever they called them on a ship.

It was obvious from the distance they'd traveled from the hold the ship was a big one. Some kind of freighter or steamer, probably, in the business of hauling stuff from one place to another. But where in the world were they?

Had Great-Uncle Henry's game sent them to some

strange place so it would be hard to get home? Marcus could hardly wait to ask the captain some questions.

He waited until the officer seated himself, gestured to the visitor's chairs.

Marcus and Samantha sat, watched the captain.

He studied them in silence for a few moments, gave a half smile, then spoke. "You know, since you've stowed away on my ship, you could be treated as pirates, don't you?"

"Pirates?" Samantha's voice was a mere squeak.

The captain scowled. "You know what happens to pirates, don't you?"

Marcus gulped. All the pirate tales he'd ever read flitted through his mind. Punishments ranging from flogging to walking the plank. Surely the man wasn't serious…was he?

## CHAPTER 7

"Trust me, mister...sir...we aren't pirates." Marcus spoke with firmness but also respect. "My sister and I aren't exactly sure how we got on board your ship, but it was an accident."

The captain's skeptical expression made Marcus want to explain further, but how could he tell the officer anything when they didn't have a clue why they were on his boat? Marcus fisted his hand in the pocket of his jeans, felt the stone he had placed there earlier and fingered the rock. The smooth coolness soothed his panic.

Silence while the captain watched them. "So you're telling me you don't know how you ended up in the corn cargo on my steamship traveling down Lake Michigan?"

Lake Michigan! Omigosh. Great-Uncle Henry's game had taken them from Texas to another state.

"Please, sir." Samantha broke into his musings. "Can you tell us what this ship is?"

The officer's face showed surprise. "You're on the *L. R. Doty*, a wooden steamship operating out of Cleveland, Ohio. I'm Captain Christopher Smith. Suppose you introduce yourselves."

Marcus spoke up. "I'm Marcus Willoughby, sir,

and this is my twin sister Samantha."

"Twins, eh? Suppose you explain why we found you in one of the holds of my ship on top of some of my corn cargo."

"Yessir. I understand you want to know that. But could you tell me a little about your ship first?" Marcus hoped if he showed an interest in the boat, the captain might look more favorably on them.

The captain huffed, but then smiled. "Technically, the *Doty* is built of white oak, with a hull length of 291 feet. We have a capacity of over 2,000 gross tons for cargo and nine deck holds to put it in. We've also got a tall foremast where we can set canvas...sails...if needed. Does that cover what you want to know?"

A twinkle in his eyes at least hinted at a sense of humor. He must have known they'd be overwhelmed with all the facts and figures.

"Wow!" Marcus tried to think of something else to ask. "Do you use the sails?"

"Not really," said the captain. "We're powered by a three-cylinder triple expansion engine."

"How does that make it move the ship?" At this point, Marcus truly began to be interested."

As if sensing that, the captain continued. "That means it can generate 1,000 horsepower at seventy-five rpm to run our huge propeller. Plus...."

Marcus had to ask. "There's more?"

The captain nodded. "We have two Scotch boilers that feed the fully equipped steam power system for our deck winches when we load and unload the corn or whatever cargo we're carrying."

"The steam is what gives you power, right?"

asked Marcus. "It provides electricity for the lights and the radio." He hoped he'd managed to derail the officer's curiosity since his own head was spinning with so much information.

The captain's laugh boomed loud. "We use tungsten filament lamps for the interior of the ship. No electric lights or radio, young man. Maybe in the future."

Samantha leaned forward. "What do you mean in the future? What is the date?"

Ha. Sami was thinking along the same lines as Marcus. He'd been ready to ask the same question.

The captain looked at the girl. "Did you two have a head injury before or after you came on board?"

A fair question. But not one that had a positive answer.

"No, sir," said Marcus. "We...we just aren't sure of the date."

"Hmmm. It's October 24th. A little after two o'clock in the afternoon."

"October 24th. That's right." Marcus exchanged a look with Samantha. "What...er...what year is it?"

The captain appeared disbelieving before he finally responded in a dry tone of voice. "It's still 1898."

"1898." The twins chorused the date.

"Yes. 1898." The captain shoved his chair away from his desk. "Look here. I think I'd better have the first mate take a look at you. He's not a doctor, but he has a little medical training. Follow me. We'll find you a cabin and let him check you over. You're beginning to worry me."

Huh! He wasn't the only one who was worried. Marcus's head was spinning with the date he'd just heard. October 24th was fine, but 1898? How many years was that from their normal life? Over a hundred. It appeared Great-Uncle Henry had not only sent them to a different place, but a different time as well.

He sensed Samantha was as bewildered and shocked as he was. They needed to talk privately so they could try to figure out what was going on and how in the world they were ever going to return to their own time and lives.

# # # #

"Does this hurt?" First Mate Henry Sharp pressed his fingers along the top and sides of Marcus's head.

The boy jerked away. "No. It tickles."

"Good." The mate gave him an approving look. "No aches or pains anywhere?"

"Nope." Marcus couldn't help it if he seemed abrupt, but he had been poked and prodded for what seemed like half an hour, after the man had checked out Samantha.

"Guess you two aren't injured. I can't find anything wrong with you."

The mate stood and moved away from the bunk where Marcus sat. "If you have any headaches or blurry vision, let me know. I'll tell Captain Smith you seem fine."

"Right." "Okay." The twins' responses blended and followed the officer as he left the room. The minute the door closed, they turned and stared at each other.

"1898?" Samantha's question reflected the shock mirrored on her face.

"And Lake Michigan?" Marcus imagined he sounded as disbelieving as his sister. "What has Great-Uncle Henry gotten us into?"

"More importantly, Marko, how can we get home?"

"Good question."

"And the answer?"

He frowned. "I don't know."

They both fell silent.

Finally, Samantha heaved a sigh. "We'd better try to find out more about where we are. Maybe we'll get some clues to help us return to our own time and place."

"It's kind of funny, Sami." Marcus again fingered the stone in his pocket. "Do you realize we've ended up on a ship? A ship a whole lot like the picture of the one on the token."

"You're right." Samantha twisted a lock of her hair, a sure sign her mind was racing. "Before we do anything else, let's try to remember exactly what happened at home before we got here, so maybe we can discover a way to get back."

Marcus relaxed on the bunk where he sat. "We were on the floor by the game board and you had your finger on the ship token and moved it toward me."

"Right." Samantha paced in a circle in the small compartment. "Then you put your finger on top of mine and we moved the token to one of the Spinning Circles. All of a sudden, I remember feeling kind of dizzy and sick. Next thing I knew, we were in the hold of the ship counting corn kernels."

"And calling cats." Marcus had to add it.

"Do you suppose our touching hands is what...triggered, I guess is the word...our being here?"

"Dunno. Obviously, Great-Uncle Henry wasn't as much of a loser as an inventor as we thought. He somehow tapped into space and time, which is a pretty smart thing to do."

Samantha assumed a thoughtful expression. "Yes. I'm sure he was smarter than we dreamed. But we've got to be smart, too, and decide how to get out of the situation we're in. Think, Marko. You've got a brain. Use it."

Marcus could tell from the sound of Samantha's voice her concern level had raised. "Calm down, Sami. We'll get back home."

"I hope it's that simple. We've got some obvious problems to overcome here...besides getting home."

"Such as?" Marcus sat back up.

"Such as the captain thinking we're nuts or that we have some underhanded motive for being on his boat. Probably both since the first mate didn't find any signs of injury."

"So what did you want me to do? Say 'ouch' when nothing hurt?" Marcus knew he was acting grumpy but it was how he felt inside. "Maybe we won't need to do any pretending." Marcus squirmed around on the bunk, put his feet on the floor. "Let's see if they'll let us explore the ship. Maybe we'll find some clues."

"Clues? What clues? This isn't a mystery we're trying to solve, Marko. We need to find a way to get home. From more than a hundred years in the past." Samantha's voice cracked as she gave a big sniff.

Uh, oh. Sami was on the verge of tears. Never a pretty sight. Marcus thought fast. How could he help her calm down? Especially since panic built inside him as well.

"Tell you what. How about if we walk around the ship, talk to some of the crew members? Maybe we'll get some ideas from being in the fresh air. I can still smell those corn kernels." He gave an exaggerated sniff. "Ugh. I may never want to eat corn-on-the-cob again."

Samantha's lips creased in a tiny grin. "Sure. Sounds good." She stood and headed for the door. "After all, we've never been on this big a ship before. It ought to be interesting to say the least."

Marcus followed her from the room. Interesting? It had to be more than interesting. They desperately needed an idea on how to get back to their own time, or they might stay aboard the *L. R. Doty* for a lot longer than they wanted. Like maybe forever.

CHAPTER 8

The twins emerged onto the deck of the *Doty*. Sailors stood in different places. Some appeared to be keeping a watch while others were busy cleaning the deck. A small group clustered at what he thought should be the back of the ship.

"Let's go down there." Marcus nudged Samantha toward the knot of sailors.

Walking toward the men, Marcus noticed them studying a thick rope partially wound around a large spool that looked like a giant fishing reel.

"Hi." Marcus figured being friendly couldn't hurt. "What's going on?"

The men jerked around. Various expressions of shock and surprise reflected on suntanned faces.

"Kids? What are kids doing here?"

"Where did you two come from?"

"A girl?"

The chorus of questions fired at them from several directions at once.

"I'm Marcus." He gestured toward his sister. "This is my twin, Samantha. We're from...another place. We're...just visiting." He hoped that was the truth.

"I'm Pat," one of them said. "How did you kids

get here? I didn't see anybody besides the crew come aboard while I was on watch."

A murmur came from the others.

"We, uh, were kind of stuck in a room when we first arrived." Marcus wanted to be truthful, but didn't want to try to explain how they had found themselves in a hold full of corn kernels. He and Samantha had a hard enough time believing it; the men probably would also. Besides, once the crew all got together for a meal all the details would get around fast enough.

"Hmmm." Pat sounded puzzled, but didn't pursue the topic. He half-turned away and gestured at the rope. "We're checking to be sure the towline is secure."

"Towline? What's being towed?" Marcus stood on tiptoe to see over the ship's railing. In the distance he could make out what appeared to be another boat. Not like the *Doty*, but one more along the lines of sailing ships he'd seen pictures of.

"That's the *Olive Jeanette*," said Pat. "She's a 242-foot, four-masted schooner barge. We're towing her to our destination in Midland, Ontario where we'll deliver our corn. The *Olive Jeanette* carries a cargo of corn too, to unload at the same place."

"Why are you towing them?" Samantha chimed in, interest and curiosity mingled in her tone. "Can't they sail by themselves?"

Pat turned toward her before he replied. "They used to be able to until they shortened the masts and made a cargo barge out of her."

Another of the men spoke up. "Now they can only

use one sail, but they don't do that very often. Only in bad weather."

The twins looked at him.

He saluted. "I'm W. J., Second Mate on the *Doty*. By using both vessels, we carry twice as much cargo. The *Olive Jeanette's* our permanent tow. We unload and re-load at the same time. Once we unload in Canada, we'll get a load of iron ore or coal, or maybe some other kind of grain and return to our home port. The *Jeanette* has a single post this 6-strand rope is tied to on their ship and we've got the other end tied to this reel here on the *Doty*.

"The line helps, too," said Pat, "so we can keep up with each other in case we run into bad weather. Then the towline will stretch and then slacken when there are heavy waves, and it could snap the towline in an instant. In the kind of storms we get here on Lake Michigan this time of year, they could have a rough go of it by themselves if a storm struck. With the load they're carrying, it would be hard for them to make it on the little bit of sail power they've got."

"Storms?" Marcus tried to sound casual. "Do you have many storms on the lake?"

The men's laughs blended in an ominous sound.

"Yeah, you could say that." A third man spoke up. "Why, when we get a storm on the lake, everything afloat is in danger. Waves taller than this ship can occur."

Marcus swallowed. "That's pretty tall."

"Yep." The man continued, obviously enjoying his narrative of disaster. "I can recall some storms where I thought we'd sink for sure."

"Stow it, George." W. J. gestured toward the others. "Everybody get to work."

He stood, hands on hips as the men drifted away to other duties. He turned toward the twins.

"You kids stay out of the way." His order was firm but made in a kind voice. "It's easy to get hurt on a ship if you don't know what you're doing."

"May we stay here on the deck?" Samantha's plea held a note of desperation.

"Sure, miss. Being on deck is fine. But don't mess with things or get in someone's way, okay?" He started to walk away. "I'll probably see you at chow."

Marcus's stomach rumbled at the familiar word. Chow. He didn't know what the time was right now, but his body knew food ought to be on the agenda soon. He squinted at the hazy sun. Too bad he couldn't tell time from its position. Regardless, it was time for a snack. It certainly felt like a long time since his last meal.

# # # #

For the next half hour or so, Marcus and Samantha wandered around the deck of the ship. As requested, they avoided interrupting the working sailors, although they received friendly acknowledgements from most of them. The *Doty's* crew appeared to be a good bunch of men.

Finally, Samantha broke the silence. "I wish we could talk to the captain or another officer again. I have some questions I want to ask."

"Me, too," said Marcus. The sharp sea breeze had

stimulated his brain cells as well as his appetite. "Maybe we can ask somebody at dinner."

Samantha considered. "Okay. I have to admit, I'm getting a bit hungry."

"I'm starving." Marcus's pointed ahead. "Look, there's Pat. Let's ask him when we eat."

They headed toward the sailor who'd first spoken to them. As they drew near, he looked up from the rope he was coiling on the deck. "Kids. You doing all right?"

"I'd be doing better if I had something to eat." Marcus rubbed his stomach.

Pat snorted a laugh, laid the last piece of rope down, studied the sky. "Good thing we always have food available. C'mon. I'll show you where the dining salon is."

"Dining salon," Marcus whispered to his sister. "My, my, aren't we fancy?"

Samantha elbowed him. "Don't be smarty. That's probably what they called a dining room on a ship a hundred years ago."

Marcus gave her a skeptical look, but they followed close at Pat's heels as the sailor led the way.

The twins hung back as they entered a long, narrow room in what seemed to be the middle of the ship. Wooden tables with benches, rather like modern picnic tables, filled the center of the room. Ropes hung from the ceiling were attached to each corner of the tabletops. What appeared to be ten or fifteen men lined the benches, laughing, talking, creating their own roar in the confined quarters.

Marcus couldn't believe his eyes. The scene

reminded him of every sea story he'd ever read. And to think, he and his sister were part of it. Excitement rose inside him as he surveyed the scene.

"You two go ahead and have a seat." Pat pointed to an empty bench. "I'll get us a snack and bring it over."

Samantha sat down on the nearest bench, Marcus across from her. They smiled at each other.

"It's like living in a storybook," whispered Samantha. She glanced around at the men seated at the nearest table.

After one quick look, they'd all gone back to their eating and ignored the twins.

"Yeah." Marcus continued to observe the seamen. "Hope they have something good to eat. I'm starved."

Pat approached, bearing three thick dishes. "Here you go." He sat the plates on the table, scooted one each in front of the brother and sister. "Dig in."

He picked up the fork balanced on the plate and raised a bite to his mouth, chewed, and swallowed. "Yum." He dug in for another portion.

After a quick taste of her own, Samantha followed suit.

Before long, their plates were clean. Marcus patted his tummy. "Boy, you have a really good cook. That pie was as good as the ones my mom makes."

Without warning, he tried to tear up. Thoughts of his mother and father, far away in time and place, clutched his heart with sudden sadness.

He checked on Samantha. Her quivering bottom lip told him she felt the same way.

Pat cleared his throat. "You kids okay?"

The twins nodded, tried for a more upbeat expression.

The sailor looked at them for a moment, then shrugged. "If you've eaten all you want, let's dump the dishes for Scotty, our cook, to wash and we'll head back on deck. I heard the captain wanted to talk to you some more."

Marcus and Samantha scooted off the benches, grabbed dishes and utensils and followed Pat to where a couple of large pans sat on a table near the doorway into the galley.

Pat scraped a few bits of food off his plate, placed it and his silverware in the other pan. He looked at the twin's plates and grinned. "Guess you two don't have any leftovers, so put your dishes in the pan and we'll head up."

They followed Pat's instructions then trailed him as he headed out the door through which they'd entered.

After a lot of walking, they climbed a short flight of stairs and came out on the deck of the *Doty*.

The formerly sunny day had turned into one with shades of gray streaking the sky.

Clouds hung low and heavy on the horizon in the fading early evening light. Thankfully it was still light enough to see their way clearly to move along the deck to the bridge.

Pat looked at the sky. "Hmmm. We may be in for a bit of a blow." He started forward. "Watch your step. The bridge is over that way."

A few minutes later, he opened a door and preceded the twins into the command center.

Captain Smith bent over a table occupying the center of the room.

At one end of the wheelhouse a sailor stood, hands on the wheel, piloting the *Doty* through the choppy waves that showed gray and swollen through the windows lining the room.

The captain nodded when he saw them. "Did you have something to eat?"

"Yes, sir." Marcus wanted to salute, but thought it might not be appropriate. "It was really good, too."

Smith chuckled. "Yep, Scotty is one good cook. I'm glad you enjoyed it."

Marcus moved forward and studied the chart that the captain held open on the table.

"Is that a map of where we are now?"

"It is. And of the entire lake all the way to where we deliver our cargo."

"The corn." Marcus said.

"Right. If all goes well, and the weather holds, we should be there day after tomorrow. Once we make port and get the corn off the ship, I'll see what I can do to help you find your folks."

"Not likely." Samantha breathed the comment from where she stood behind Marcus.

He wheeled and glared at her. They needed to be careful.

The last thing they wanted was for the captain and crew to learn they weren't only from a different place...but they'd also come from a different time.

If they claimed to be from the future, no telling what the captain would do.

Marcus wondered if there were jail cells on ships

in 1898.

He sure didn't want to find out.

CHAPTER 9

"I know a map won't make sense to you two since you're landlubbers." The captain's grin robbed the term of any offense. "Why don't you tell me what you remember about getting on my ship?"

Marcus and Samantha exchanged a long look. One of their 'twin communications' where each knew what the other had in mind without saying a word.

Marcus cleared his throat. "Uh…one minute I was thinking about a ship that could have been this one…and…and…the next thing I knew we were here."

Ouch. Not good. So close to what really occurred it wasn't an untruth, but maybe too much to tell the captain.

A puzzled frown creased the officer's brow. He turned to Samantha. "What about you little lady? Do you remember anything?"

She assumed a vague expression and shrugged. "Like Marcus said." She clamped her lips tight to avoid any other words escaping.

Frustration edged the captain's face. "That's the best you can remember? You were looking at a picture of a ship and all of a sudden you were here?"

They both nodded.

He sighed. "It doesn't make any sense." He studied them for a moment, then a kind smile curled the corners of his mouth. "I guess you kids can't be blamed for not remembering exactly what happened. If I ended up on a ship I wasn't familiar with, I'd have a problem recalling details, too."

Captain Smith gestured toward the door. "Why don't we wait on this conversation a while? Maybe something more about how you got here will come to you later. You probably need to settle down a bit before dinner."

"Yes, sir. We'll do that," said Marcus.

"Mind you don't get too close to the outside edge of the ship." The captain sounded concerned. "You could be overboard in an instant and these waters are too rough for someone your size to be able to swim in for long."

Samantha's gulp could be heard in the stillness following the man's pronouncement.

Marcus nodded. "We'll be careful."

"Go ahead, then." The captain turned his attention back to the chart in front of him.

Marcus and Samantha exited the bridge and stood outside.

"Which direction shall we go?" Samantha's voice broke into Marcus's thinking.

He shrugged. "Doesn't matter. We'll see both ends at some point."

Samantha chuckled. "True. It's not exactly an endless walk, is it?" She turned right. "C'mon. Let's go this way first."

They headed toward the front of the boat, again

passing sailors who were busy with various chores.

After a few minutes, Samantha stopped and faced Marcus. "What are we going to do, Marko? If the captain keeps asking us questions, we're either going to be forced to lie to him or play really dumb, which is kind of a lie, too. I mean, we do know what happened, we just don't know exactly how it all came about."

Marcus thought for a moment. "We probably need to keep out of his way as much as possible, Sami. If he doesn't see us, he can't ask questions."

"Okay. Let's look around. After all, it's not everyone who gets stuck on an 1898 sailing vessel. It's a real adventure, you have to admit."

He grinned. "True." He made a couple of passes with an imaginary sword. "If this were a pirate ship, I could have all kinds of fun."

"Right. They'd probably put you in jail in their brig. Get real, brother. We may be in a different century than our own, but we are in the middle of Lake Michigan. I don't think there were too many pirates here in 1898."

"There might have been. Wouldn't it be great if we ran across one now?" Marcus made another lunge at a nonexistent enemy.

Samantha beckoned. "Come on. Let's walk over here and sit down a bit. I'm a little queasy after eating that pie. Those waves aren't helping any."

They both turned and gazed at the churning lake. Even though the waves were no more than a few feet high, they were big enough to give them an idea of what it might look like if a storm struck.

Finding a large crate shoved against the backside of one of the cargo holds, they perched on the box.

Marcus nudged Samantha in the ribs. "Look, Sami. What do you suppose he's doing?"

Samantha looked to where Marcus pointed. A short, thin man, about the size of a teenager, crept across the deck fifty feet ahead of them. From where they were sitting, they had a clear view of him, but because they were sheltered by the hold he couldn't see them.

"Maybe he's some kind of lookout."

Samantha snorted. "Sneaking along the deck? Besides, lookouts would be somewhere high. Not down here."

They watched as the man edged around a couple of barrels lashed to the deck and disappeared from view.

"Huh." Marcus couldn't help wondering what the man was doing. Neither he nor his twin knew much about ships and the way they operated. Especially ones more than a hundred years old. "Maybe he's up to no good."

Samantha made a face. "Quit trying to make a mystery out of everything. He's probably being careful about how he's walking. The deck is pitching around a good bit."

Marcus noticed the motion of the boat had increased in the last few minutes. He stood. "Maybe we should go below, Sami." He put a hand on his stomach. "I'm not feeling so good."

The twins made their way carefully to the doorway leading to the interior of the ship.

Without making any wrong turns, they arrived at the cabin they'd been in earlier when the first mate had examined them for injuries.

Once inside, they sat on their bunks and stared at each other.

Samantha swallowed. "I hope we're not going to be seasick. I've read it's really bad."

"Yeah. Me, too." Marcus leaned back against the pillow. "Maybe we'll be better now we're inside and can't see the water."

"Maybe so. I don't want to be getting sick all over this room."

"There's a pretty thought." Marcus glared at her. "Let's take it easy for a while. I sure feel funny."

"I'll try," said Samantha. "But if you think you're going to throw up, please turn your head away from me."

Marcus ignored her and sank back onto the bunk. Maybe he'd take a little nap. After all, how bad could he feel since he was inside the ship where he couldn't see the waves?

CHAPTER 10

An hour later, Marcus knew the answer. Nausea clawed its way from his stomach to his throat. He gagged. Liquid tried to force its way into his mouth.

"Oh-h-h-h." He couldn't help the moan. He raised his head and looked toward his sister, hoping for some sympathy.

Instead, he saw Samantha's face had turned pale green and was covered with droplets of sweat.

"Sami," he gasped, swallowing hard. "Are you okay?"

"Just dandy."

"I think I'm going to be sick." Marcus clutched his middle with his hands, rolled over toward the wall and fought against the rising tide of nausea.

"I can't help you," Samantha moaned. "I know I'm going to be sick."

Marcus cringed as he heard sounds that could only indicate Sami had emptied her stomach. He hoped she hadn't made too big of a mess.

"Ick." Samantha's response to her illness was heartfelt. "I'm so nauseated."

Marcus didn't respond since he was in the throes of losing his own pie. Fortunately, on the floor of the cabin, not all over himself.

A few minutes later, a brief knock sounded and the door swung open. First Mate Sharp stood there, a pail and mop in his hands. "I was afraid this might happen when I saw you two leave the deck." He walked inside and closed the door. "You kids haven't been on ships before, have you?"

Marcus merely groaned. Within a few seconds, the mate sponged their faces, mopped up the mess they'd made, had them swallow a potion he said would help, and settled back on a third bunk to watch over them.

Silence reigned for some time, broken only occasionally by a moan or groan from one of the twins. Half an hour or so passed.

Sharp stood up and stretched. "You kids any better?" he asked.

Marcus was amazed to find out he was. "I think I'm gonna live." His humorous tone reflected his improvement.

"How about you, little lady?"

She nodded. "Me, too."

He rose. "Then I'll leave you and go check on a couple of other things. If you feel like dinner, it'll be in about half an hour. You know where the dining salon is. Come on there when you hear some bells ring."

Sharp opened the cabin door. A gray cat slinked in, wove its way around the mate's ankles. "Whoa." Sharp bent down and turned the cat around, gently shoved it out the door.

"Cats again?" Marcus couldn't believe the animals roamed the ship.

"Only two to keep the critters down." Sharp stepped through the doorway and exited without any further words.

Samantha watched him walk out the door, then turned toward her brother. "Marko, I've been thinking...."

"While you were losing your pie?"

"Hush. I'm wondering about the sailor we saw earlier. The one who acted like he was sneaking around on deck."

"Yeah. What about him?"

"I suspect he may be up to no good."

"Why would you think so?"

Marcus shifted to be able to look more directly at his sister. "We only saw him for a few minutes. He's probably just a member of the crew we haven't seen before."

"Maybe. But there was something about the way he was acting...."

"Samantha Willoughby, you're being ridiculous. For somebody who's usually logical and analyzes everything, when your imagination takes over, you really get carried away."

His twin glared at him. "Say what you want to, but I think he's hiding something."

"Right. Tell you what. When we go for dinner...." Marcus paused, realized after being so sick, food actually didn't sound half bad.

"We'll ask some of the other crew members who he is. Or, if he's there, we can talk to him directly."

"Oh, all right." Samantha said. "We'll wait and do it your way. But you mark my words. He's acting strange and I don't trust him a bit. You'll see."

CHAPTER 11

Captain Smith turned to the pilot with whom he shared the bridge. "Peterson, keep a sharp eye on this weather. I don't like the looks of that sky."

"Aye, aye, Captain. These waves do seem to be gettin' bigger all the time."

"I know. Keep her steady as she goes."

"Yessir." The pilot fell silent, spoke a few minutes later. "Captain, what about the *Olive Jeanette*?"

Smith sighed. "I've been thinking about her. As far as we can tell from our inspection earlier, the towline between our vessels is still in good condition. If we get a bad storm, though, it could break and they'd be on their own. We might even have to sever the line if we get in trouble so we don't cause them problems."

"Too bad we don't have some way to let them know if we need to do that."

"In such weather, there'd be no way they could see signal flags, especially if it occurred at night...so we couldn't send them such a message." The captain sighed. "We'll have to hope for the best. Maybe we can keep both vessels afloat until any storm lets up."

"Yessir. Those waves are gettin' higher by the minute, it seems. And that wind's increasin', too."

"Steady as she goes, Peterson." Smith straightened

his shoulders. "Steady as she goes."

# # # #

An hour later, bells resounded throughout the interior of the ship. Dinner time. Marcus and Samantha were prompt to find the dining salon.

Even being below decks, the ship's motion could be felt through the vibrations of its engines. Fortunately, the twins had adjusted to the movements of the rougher weather and now had no problem being ready for a meal.

To their surprise, only a few of the crew sat at the long tables.

"Where is everybody?" Marcus half-turned toward the doorway expecting to see the rest of the crew.

"Maybe we're late." Samantha's frown indicated her clear displeasure. "We can't talk to many people, or find our mystery man, if hardly anyone is here."

Marcus shrugged. "Maybe more people will show up later. Let's get some food."

They moved toward the window where they could see Scotty, the cook, moving around the galley. He turned as they walked up and headed in their direction. "You kids ready for a meal?"

"Yessir." Marcus couldn't help his eagerness. "I'm as hollow as…as…well, I'm hollow."

The cook reached for a plate and filled it. "There you are. My famous shipwreck stew."

"Yum. Smells great." Marcus gathered utensils and helped himself to a couple of cornbread squares.

He walked to the nearest table so he could be close by if a second helping was needed.

Samantha joined him, her plate containing a smaller portion. "You must really be hungry, Marko. If you eat too much, though, you might be sick again."

"Don't be silly. I'm fine. Just took me a little while to get my sea legs."

"Right." Samantha seated herself across from him, bowed her head in a brief blessing, then picked up her fork. "Remember what I said if later I'm proved correct."

Marcus ignored her and continued to wolf down his food.

After finishing half his plateful, he paused. "I've been doing some thinking, Sami, and I'm wondering if we can figure a way to get off the boat."

"Ship...it's a ship."

"Ship, boat, whatever." Marcus heaved a sigh. "Anyway...if the weather gets as bad as First Mate Sharp said it might, who knows what will happen to this vessel? I mean, it could have sunk back in 1898.

"If it did, what happens to us? Do we go down with the ship...literally? Or would we somehow be transported again to our own time and place?"

She pondered. "I don't know, Marko. I mean, since we're physically here on the ship, if it sinks, I guess we'd sink with it."

Marcus sat silent before he spoke again. "Mom and Dad would never know where or how we disappeared."

"I guess not." Samantha's lower lip quivered.

They stared at each other for a few minutes.

"Don't worry. It's not likely." Marcus tried to speak in a cheerful tone. "There are lots of sailors on the ship who know what to do in bad weather. And a captain who's experienced as well. So we shouldn't worry. Right?"

Samantha studied him, gave a slow nod. "Right. Besides, it's all in God's hands, anyway, isn't it?"

Relief flooded Marcus. "Of course it is. I'd forgotten for a minute. Thanks, Sami. Since God's in control...even in our lives in 1898, we don't have to worry. He'll take care of us."

They smiled at each other, peace restored.

Marcus rose. "I need some more stew."

# # # #

Marcus and Samantha lingered over their food, but only a few other crew members showed up. The twins tried talking to those who did, but the men ate fast, acted preoccupied and quickly left the room. No one responded to their question about the short, thin man seen on deck.

"Let's go, Marcus." Samantha walked toward the door. "We aren't getting any useful information here. Let's peek outside. Maybe we can go back to the bridge and talk to Captain Smith. He certainly knows his crew members and can tell us who our mystery man is."

"Good thought." Marcus followed her from the salon.

They headed for the stairs leading to the deck.

Once there, they tried to open the heavy door. It didn't budge.

"Wow." Marcus strained to push it open. "This door must face the wind. I guess the wind's picked up some. There's no way we're going to get out here."

"Phooey." Disgust was plainly in Samantha's voice. "Isn't there another door leading to the deck? Maybe we can make it to the other side of the ship and find a door not facing the wind."

"Maybe." Marcus turned slowly in all directions. "Let's take this corridor and see where it leads."

They started off. After walking for what seemed like a long time, winding their way around and around, they finally arrived at another set of stairs leading to a doorway.

"Maybe that's a way out." Samantha's relief was obvious.

"I hope so." Marcus passed her and climbed the stairs first. "I didn't think we'd ever find another exit."

"It's worse than a maze. Here...." Samantha placed her hands on the door alongside his. "Let's see if we can open it."

They both pulled, then pushed, trying to move the heavy door. With a creak and a groan, it opened a few inches.

Marcus peered out the slit. "I can't see anything, Sami. It's getting dark. The sun's about down."

Samantha shoved him aside, looked for herself. "Hmmm. I see what you mean. Let's see if we can get it open some more."

The twins shoved with all their might. The door

moved outward a few more inches. Enough to give them a better view of what was outside, but not enough for them to squeeze through.

Samantha peeked out again, gasped, turned to Marcus. "Marko, there he is again. The man we saw before."

He shouldered her aside. "Where? Let me see."

Marcus peered through the opening, caught a glimpse of the man, or at least the man's back. "He's carrying something."

"What?"

"Don't know. Can't tell. Some kind of bag. He was heading toward the hatches. If he doesn't blow away first. He's awfully little to be out in the storm."

"Hey, you kids."

The shout from the stair bottom caught them by surprise.

A crew member stood there, a huge scowl on his face. "Get the door closed. We don't need spray in here."

They tried to pull it shut, but didn't have the strength to budge it.

"Here," the man took the stairs two at a time and moved them aside, "let me do that."

Muscles knotted and strained beneath his shirt as he grasped the door and slowly pulled it shut. After fastening a bar across it, he looked at the twins. "What were you two thinking? You could have been sucked outside and blown away. In this storm, nobody would have known."

"We were just curious." Samantha's words contained a bit of a whine.

"Well, no more opening doors. No one is going outside this time of day unless they're on duty. Most of the crew is in their cabins. You need to head to yours."

"But there was someone out there." Samantha blurted out the words.

The sailor shook his head. "No way. The deck crew's been gone for half an hour."

Marcus decided he needed to chime in. "I saw him, too. It was the little guy, the one about the size of a teenager. He was carrying a bag...."

"You kids have great imaginations, I'll give you that." The seaman shook his head, a sort of admiration showing on his face. "Enough pretending. Head on to your cabin and stay there until morning."

"But...."

The seaman gently grasped their upper arms and steered them down the stairs and into the corridor.

"Go on. You'll be safe in your cabin until time for breakfast."

He stood and watched as they walked away from him.

Samantha grumbled under her breath the whole way. "We know we saw the little man again. And I bet he's up to no good."

Marcus had trouble keeping up with her fast pace. "I saw him, too, Sami. It's funny, though, the crewman didn't seem to recognize our description of the guy. Surely the crew all knows each other."

They stood silent.

Samantha twirled a lock of her hair before she slowly responded. "Unless he isn't a member of the crew and they don't know he's on board."

CHAPTER 12

Marcus sucked in a breath. "Wow. That would explain a lot."

"Yeah, but what's an outsider doing on this ship and why is he trying to avoid being seen? If it's so late to be on deck, he's taking a chance of being spotted by the crew if he's walking around."

"Unless he has a powerful reason." Marcus's mind raced through several scenarios. "I can think of a lot of possibilities for his secrecy."

"So can I," snapped Samantha. "But if we can't find anyone to talk to us about him, we'll never know the answer."

They continued toward their cabin. When they reached the door, Marcus shoved it open, let his sister go in first.

The twins sat on their respective bunks, stared at the floor, then at each other.

Finally, Samantha spoke. "So what are we going to do?"

Marcus shrugged. "I don't think we can do anything, Sami. We're going to have to wait until morning, then maybe we can spot the guy again and catch him doing whatever he's trying to do. No bigger than he is, together we could probably grab him and hold him until one of the sailors arrives to help."

She tugged her hair, sighed. "I guess. It's frustrating, though. I have a really bad feeling about the guy. I wish the captain or one of the other officers would take us seriously."

"Yeah, but it's not going to happen. They think we're just imagining things. Let's see what's going on by breakfast. Maybe we can try again with our questions, or at least, get somebody to listen to us about our mystery man."

"Right." Samantha stretched out on her bunk. "In that case, I'm going to bed. Wake me when it's time for breakfast."

"Hmmph." Marcus studied his sister. "Go ahead and sleep. I'll stay awake for a while and try to figure a way to catch MM...Mystery Man...while you snooze."

"Mmmm." Samantha's drowsy murmur was her only response.

Marcus watched her for a moment. When she began to breathe in an even rhythm, he snorted in disgust, stretched out on his own bunk, hands clasped behind his head. Fine. He'd do his own detecting. Who knew? Maybe he'd have a solution ready to propose by breakfast.

# # # #

Breakfast didn't prove any more profitable for interviews than had the previous day. The sailors ate in a hurry and headed to their posts.

After lingering in the dining salon long past the time they finished eating, Marcus stood.

"We're not going to get any info here, Sami. Let's dump the dishes and go on deck. We can stroll along and look at every crew member we meet. If mystery man works on the ship we should see him."

"Good thinking." Samantha gathered her dishes and walked toward the utility pan near the galley. "We've got all day to look around.

The twins were soon on deck, heading toward the end of the ship where the boiler room and smokestack were located.

Taking their time, they peered closely at every crew member they saw. None of them was the mystery man.

During their walk back, they split up and walked around all the cargo holds in case the man they sought might be on his knees doing some chore.

Still no sign of him.

Samantha turned to Marcus as they finished the second trip the length of the ship.

"Marko, I'm tired. Either we need to find a spot where we can sit down and rest here on the deck or go back to the cabin."

"Our MM is pretty good at remaining unseen," said Marcus, ignoring Samantha's desire to rest. "I'm beginning to agree he's not a member of the crew. One of the sailors shouldn't be this hard to find if he really works here."

Samantha shivered. "The wind is blowing harder, too, and I'm getting cold. Maybe that storm First Mate Sharp mentioned is coming in."

Marcus nodded. "I vote for the cabin. It shouldn't be that long until lunch. We can make that our last try for information from the crew – or for spotting our MM."

"Let's go." Samantha started down the deck toward the main staircase door. "The cabin's sounding better all the time."

# # # #

The next couple of hours dragged by as the twins discussed the MM, the possibilities of a storm, and even ways they might be able to return home.

Worn out with boredom and an underlying fear of what the future held, they both fell asleep.

# # # #

Marcus's eyelids popped open. Oh, no. He hadn't meant to take a nap. He looked at Samantha's bunk. She still slept, a slight whiffle escaping her lips from time to time.

His stomach growled once, then again. What time was it? Had they missed lunch? He hadn't heard a bell, but maybe he'd been sleeping too soundly to notice.

A third growl moved him to action. Swinging his feet off the mattress, he leaned across to Samantha's bunk and shook her shoulder.

"Sami, wake up. We may have slept through lunch."

After a few more attempts to awaken her,

Samantha's eyelids fluttered open. "Marko. What...what's going on?"

"C'mon, Sis. We're either late for lunch or we've missed it entirely. Let's head for the dining salon. I'm starving."

Samantha's stomach rumble harmonized with another one of his.

They both stood, straightened their rumpled clothes.

"Let's go." Marcus opened the door and led the way. As he stepped into the corridor, the ship pitched more violently than ever.

"Whoa. That storm must have hit while we were asleep." Marcus grabbed at the door frame to steady himself. "Be careful, sis. I think we're about to experience an adventure."

As they reached the dining salon entrance, two of the crew members exited.

"Got us a first-class blow out there," one sailor said to the other.

"Yep. At the rate it's increasing, it's like a hurricane," responded the other man. "Be nice if there was an eye we could get to before long and have some relief from the wind, sleet, and snow."

They left as Marcus and Samantha entered the salon.

Samantha turned toward her brother, excitement on her face. "Marko, did you hear? If it's truly a hurricane, maybe when we hit the eye, we can catch our mystery man."

"Just keep calling him MM," said Marcus. "It's faster."

Samantha quirked a grin at him. "You just have to be cute-sy, don't you?"

"Merely trying to keep things clear," he said. "Seriously, Sami, let's see if we can get an answer from one of the mates, or the captain, about how long it may be before the 'eye' thing hits. We need to be sure we'll be awake if it's in the middle of the night, for instance. It'd be a shame to miss our MM because we were snoozing again."

"Good point." She looked around the room at the partially occupied tables. "I don't see either First Mate Sharp or Second Mate Bossie, do you?"

"Not yet." Even as Marcus said the words, the door to the dining salon opened and First Mate Sharp entered. "Ha, there's our officer."

The twins waited until Sharp had obtained a plateful of food and seated himself at one of the tables. They walked over to where he gulped the meal.

"First Mate?" Marcus projected his voice louder than usual, aware the man was probably preoccupied with the situation of the ship.

Sharp gave a startled upward glance. "Kids? Are you two doing okay?"

"Yes, sir." Marcus didn't wait. "Sir, we heard someone say we're in a hurricane and the eye would give us some relief from the wind and waves. Is that true?"

The first mate paused eating. "Where did you hear that?"

"One of the sailors said something about it." Marcus tried again. "Is it a hurricane?"

Sharp's impatient shake of his head provided the answer. "We don't have hurricanes on the Great Lakes, Marcus. It's probably what's called an extratropical cyclone. Sometimes they're called a November gale or a November witch." He winked. "Even if it's only October."

"So there won't be anything like the eye of a hurricane where everything gets still for a while before it hits again?"

The mate shrugged. "Usually these storms can maintain hurricane-force wind gusts, produce waves over fifty feet high and dump several inches of rain or feet of snow. They can stay over the Great Lakes for hours or days."

Marcus's shoulders slumped and he avoided Sharp's gaze.

The man continued. "Sometimes we do have what's called a "sucker hole" – a false lull in the storm. If a captain doesn't know better, he might think the whole weather thing is over…but it's what I said…a lull. The storm will hit again in full force or worse. It's been an unusually active fall weather-wise and this storm is really different."

Sharp shoved away from the table and picked up his empty plate. "You kids need to stay below deck until we get a lull…if we do. If it's safe to come topside, somebody'll let you know. Meanwhile, I've got to return to the wheelhouse and relieve the captain. I'll also have one of the crew bring you a couple of jackets to keep you warm. This storm is going to cool things off in a hurry, even below deck."

"Yessir." Marcus tried to contain his inner

excitement. So there was a possibility a lull could happen. Perhaps if it did, he and his sister could do some more investigating. It didn't appear they would get any help from the crew or officers. Too much going on with the storm. But he and Samantha would stay alert. There might be an opportunity after all to find their MM.

CHAPTER 13

Marcus and Samantha spent the next couple of hours hovering between staircases leading to doorways and their cabin. The promised jackets had been delivered and the twins had been glad of the warmer clothing. Several sailors pushed by them, entering and exiting to the outside.

Each time the door opened a flurry of snow and ice came with it.

Finally, about mid-afternoon, a sailor came through the doorway where the twins stood. No ice or snow accompanied him, nor was there any sound of the gale that had blown for what seemed like forever. The ship's motion had also calmed.

"Is the storm over?" Marcus's eager question stopped the sailor in mid-step.

"Nay…not over. Cap'n says it's gotta be one of them sucker holes. We'll take it any way we can get it. We're gonna try to pour on the steam and get further down the lake before it hits…."

"So is it safe for us to go on deck?" Samantha pointed upward.

He shrugged. "Dunno. Not my decision. Guess you can ask the cap'n. He's on the bridge." The man walked away.

Marcus and Samantha looked at each other, gave each other a high five.

"Let's go." Marcus charged up the stairway, Samantha only a step or two behind.

Shoving the now easily-opened door, they burst onto the deck, skidded to a stop. No sunshine, but at least no wind and no snow or sleet. Ice lay over the hatches, but even so it was a relief to be outside again.

"What do we do?" Marcus carefully negotiated an icy patch. "Shall we try to find the captain and ask some questions about our MM? Or do we snoop around and try to find him ourselves?"

She looked thoughtful. "Let's check around a bit first. If we find him, maybe we can shout for some of the crew to come capture him and take him to the captain for answers."

"Right." Marcus wheeled and marched toward the nearest hatch where snow lay piled on top of the cover. "I don't suppose we'll find him inside the hatches. With so much snow on top of them, no one could have gotten inside."

Samantha shuddered. "Nobody would want to be inside with all the corn. They wouldn't be able to move safely."

"True." Marcus made a slow 360 turn, scrutinizing each direction. "So where do you think someone would hide if he was trying to stay out of sight?"

"Hmmm." Samantha stood there for a moment, twirling a lock of hair. "What about the engine room? The boiler room? Whatever they call it?"

Marcus thought. "Good idea, but wouldn't the crew have discovered him? I mean, they've probably had to go in there during the storm to check on things."

"Good point." Samantha made her own survey of the deck. "I guess he could have gotten inside and hidden in an empty cabin or under a staircase. Maybe we should check and see how many doors lead to the deck and check them out. See if there's any sign someone has been lurking in those areas."

"Okay." Marcus started to walk away, stopped. "You want to stay together or investigate separately?"

She considered. "We probably should stick with each other. If we find the guy it may take both of us to grab him to keep him from getting away." Samantha marched forward. "We need to hurry, Marcus. The storm could start again at any time." She gave a nervous glance over her shoulder. "Those clouds are still awfully dark."

"Right. Lead the way. I'm right behind you."

The two swiftly made their way to the nearest door, opened it, descended a few steps on the staircase leading inside the ship. No obvious signs of anyone else were present.

A second staircase, then a third, yielded no results as well.

"One more door and we're back to the engine room," grumbled Marcus. "Here, let's check this last staircase, Sami."

The two heaved the door, the one furthest from the view of the bridge, opened it and went down several steps.

"I don't see...." Samantha stopped, leaned forward, peered beneath the stairs. "Wait. What's that?" She clattered down the staircase. "Stay there by the door, Marko, and hold it open so I have better light."

A minute later, she re-appeared, bearing an assortment of pieces of paper and one crust of a stale roll. She joined Marcus by the door.

"Look. Somebody's been there. They obviously had food and left some trash."

"Great spotting, Sami." Marcus patted her shoulder. "It must be our guy."

"Yes. And he could be anywhere. I mean, the ship is over 200 feet long and 40 feet wide. How can we search the whole thing? Especially before the storm strikes again?"

"We'll have to find a spot on deck where we can hide." Marcus looked around. "We've seen him several times outside. I can't figure if he's up to something or trying to find a way to get off the ship."

He stiffened. "Sami, what about the lifeboats? If the guy wants to escape wouldn't he need a boat?"

"He sure would. Good thinking, Marko. Let's see where the lifeboats are and try to find a place to hide near them. That way, we'll be able to find our MM if he shows. It's logical with a lull in the storm, if he's going to get off the ship, now would be the time."

"Right. C'mon, sis. I remember seeing where the lifeboats are."

The twins ran back up the staircase and onto the deck.

"This way." Marcus pointed. "Follow me."

He charged forward, Samantha close behind.

A few minutes later, they stopped. Several

lifeboats sat on the deck. One hung halfway off the side, obviously ripped from the restraints usually holding it on deck.

Marcus studied the situation. One of the holds was only a few feet away. "Here." He led the way around the hold and squatted down. The hold and its hatch cover were high enough to hide them from sight.

Samantha's panting slowed as she stopped hurrying. "Now what?"

"Now," said Marcus. "We wait."

CHAPTER 14

"How long have we been here?" Samantha's whispered question warmed the back of Marcus's neck.

"At least ten or fifteen minutes," he said. He tried to stifle a groan. "I'm really getting stiff from crouching."

"Me, too," said Samantha. "I don't know if I can stand or not. At least not in a hurry."

They fell silent. A moment later, the sound of shuffling feet sounded on the deck.

Samantha grasped Marcus's upper arm and squeezed. He nodded. He'd heard it, too. He peeked around the corner of the hatch wall.

A thin, small figure walked toward the lifeboats.

"It's him." Samantha's hiss blasted in Marcus's ear.

He half-turned, geared down his voice. "Wait until he gets closer to the boats, then we'll jump out and confront him."

Samantha drew in a breath.

They stayed quiet and waited as the MM drew nearer the boats.

As the man reached for a boat, Marcus stood. He tried to hurry forward, but his benumbed feet kept him from moving very fast. "Hey, mister. We want to talk to you."

The man glanced over his shoulder and scrambled forward, tried to reach the first boat.

"Wait." Marcus almost caught up with him. "Stop."

The man started to climb over the side into the lifeboat.

"Stop." Samantha joined the chase. "Who are you and what are you doing on this ship?"

The man froze, whirled toward them. His hand darted to his waistband and he pulled a knife from it. "Stay back."

"Easy, mister." Marcus's voice cracked a little. "You don't need to pull a knife on us."

"Who are you?" The man snarled the question from a face set in an unfriendly expression. "What do you want with me?"

Marcus retreated a step. "We want to know why you're on the ship."

"I'm one of the crew."

Samantha spoke up. "No, you're not. Nobody knows who you are. We asked."

Marcus cringed. He wished Sami hadn't given out that information.

"Nobody knows I'm on board, huh?" The look that creased the man's face was pure evil. He cackled. "Good. Then they won't be expecting my little surprise."

"What surprise?" Marcus figured he needed to get back into the conversation.

"Don't you wish you knew?" The man waved the

knife toward them. "You two may be useful, even so. Get over here and help me lower that boat."

Marcus stared at him. "I don't know anything about launching lifeboats, and neither does she." He gestured toward Samantha.

The man glared at them before he responded. "Then help me push the one that's hanging halfway over the side the rest of the way off."

Marcus and Samantha did some 'twin communication', moved forward to place their hands on the rear of the lifeboat where it barely rested on the deck.

"Push." The man's order came through loud and clear.

The twins pushed as hard as they could, but the heavy boat barely budged.

"We...can't...move it by ourselves. The thing's twelve or thirteen feet long." Marcus stood erect, glared at the man. "You want the boat off, you have to help."

MM studied his face, then thrust the knife back into his waistband. "All right, but no tricks. I can still draw my knife faster than you can move."

"No tricks," said Marcus. "You get in your boat and go away. Nobody gets hurt."

MM gave a ghoulish grin. "Not until they hear my little present.'"

Samantha's loud gulp preceded her words. "What do you mean?"

The man snickered. "Just what I said. I've left a little something for the captain on his precious ship. Won't be long, and if the storm doesn't finish them off, my bomb will."

"You can't do that." Marcus's protest sounded weak even to his own ears.

"Sure I can. What's to stop me?"

Marcus squared his shoulders. "We will."

The MM considered. "Hmmm. Yep. You two would probably run to the captain the minute I leave the ship and warn him. Not likely they'd find my package…but…you both need to come with me."

"I'm not getting in that boat." Samantha backed away, hands raised to shoulder level.

"Me neither," declared Marcus. "You leave. We stay here."

"Nope." MM waved his hand. "You two push, I push, we all leave."

"Wait." Marcus's mind worked rapidly. "Why are you doing this? What did the captain ever do to you?"

Anger crossed the MM's face. "Oh, nothing. Nothing except fire me from his crew and spread lies about me so I can't get a job anywhere else." He chuckled. "But I'll teach him a lesson. He won't have a job, either, if I blow up his precious ship. Nobody's going to trust a captain who lost his vessel."

Marcus gave the man a long look. "You're crazy."

MM's hand slapped against Marcus's jaw. "Shut up, kid. Now, you and the girl get over here and push. Now."

Ears ringing from the blow, Marcus stepped forward, placed his hands on the back of the lifeboat. Samantha followed suit.

The man joined them and the three shoved hard.

The lifeboat tilted, then slid off the deck headed to the water below. It dropped into the lake, a huge plume of spray attesting to its landing.

"Good." MM pulled the knife again. "Now you two."

"What?" Marcus almost screamed the question. "You want us to jump overboard?"

"You can climb down the ladder to get to the water. You first, then the girl. And remember, I won't hesitate to use the knife. You get in the lifeboat and help us in."

"I...I don't think I can climb down." Samantha's comment drew the man's attention.

"You'd better, kid, or this guy's in trouble."

"No. No. I'll do it." Samantha grew several shades paler. "Don't hurt my brother."

"Brother, huh? Then you jump, brother. And remember, I've got a knife next to your sister."

"I'll remember." Marcus gritted. "Don't hurt her."

The man gestured with his weapon. "Go."

Marcus moved to the side of the ship, turned toward his sister. "It's okay, Sami. We'll be okay. Do what he says."

She nodded, her teeth obviously chattering, either from fear or cold or both.

He gave her one more glance, placed his feet on the ladder and headed downward.

CHAPTER 15

Samantha watched, held her breath, as Marcus slowly lowered himself, firmly placing one foot at a time on the swaying ladder before moving to the next rung. When he reached the end of the ladder, he hesitated, then jumped into the water.

She caught her breath. They were both good swimmers, but she knew the water had to be cold.

Marcus reached the boat, grabbed it and tried to pull himself over the side into the vessel. It took three tries before the blowing wind and swelling waves let him tumble into the lifeboat. He shook himself. Water droplets flew in all directions.

"Hurry up." The MM's shout was discreet but sincere. "Get the boat over here."

Marcus picked up one of the oars and tried to paddle with it. The boat turned in a semi-circle.

Samantha heard the MM curse under his breath. He turned toward her and shoved her toward the railing. "Get on the ladder and into the boat before your stupid brother capsizes it."

"He's not stupid." Samantha glared at the MM.

"Fine. So he's not stupid. He sure doesn't know anything about rowing." The MM shoved her again. "Move."

She walked to the side of the boat, and swung her feet to the first rung of the ladder. Gulping down fear, she carefully grasped the rungs and step by step climbed downward to where Marcus and the lifeboat waited.

A few seconds later, she reached the last rung, looked over her shoulder at Marcus.

"C'mon, sis. Drop off and swim over here. I'll help you into the boat."

"Faster." The MM interrupted Marcus's words of encouragement. The guy had climbed to where Samantha's hands rested on the ladder rung above her head. "Let go, kid. Get in the boat."

Samantha glared at him, but dropped into the water. The cold liquid hit her body with the force of a blow. She struggled to rise. Breaking through the surface, she saw the lifeboat only a few feet away. Stroking, she managed to swim to its side. Her soaked clothing and shoes weighed her down.

Marcus reached over and caught one of her hands. "Here, Sami. Grab hold." As he leaned farther forward, the boat tilted.

"Stop, Marko. You're going to turn us over. You get on the other side. I can pull myself up."

The MM snickered. "And when you do, move over on the same side, girl, or I might have to hurt your brother to add some dead weight to keep things steady."

Samantha placed her hands on the side of the boat and pulled herself from the water and into the bottom of the vessel.

"Move."

The reminder from the MM caused her to scramble to where Marcus leaned against the other side of the boat.

When she reached him, he put his arm around her. They both shivered in the cold. "Are you okay?"

She nodded.

The MM heaved himself into the lifeboat and knelt, dripping, while he took deep breaths.

In only a few seconds, he roused, pulled the knife out again and waved it at them. "Okay. You two get on the oars. We're going for a little trip."

Marcus thought fast. They needed a chance to escape. Giving quick glances around the boat, he spied something under one of the seats.

"Can we at least have a life preserver to put on?" He gestured. "There are some here."

"Get them out."

Marcus edged forward and pulled on the ring he'd spotted. A cork circle came out. He fumbled around, found a second one. "Here's another." He reached under the seat a third time, felt in all directions, but couldn't find another ring. "Is there one down there where you are, mister?" He looked at the MM who sat at the opposite end of the boat watching him.

The man checked behind his feet. "Nope. There aren't any. Toss me one of yours."

Marcus considered throwing one at him and hoping it would knock the man into the water, but hesitated. If he missed, or the man stabbed at them with the knife, somebody would get hurt. He'd better cooperate for now.

Taking one of the rings, he gently tossed it toward the MM.

"Thanks." With a satisfied smirk, the man pulled the ring over his head and settled it under his arms. "Guess you kids will have to share."

His smile was anything but pleasant.

Marcus glared at him, then turned toward his sister. "Put the other one on, Sami."

"But, Marko...."

"Do it. We can share if we need to."

After studying his face for a minute, she reached for the life preserver and slowly placed it over her head and under her arms.

"Now what, mister?" Marcus scooted closer to Samantha.

"Now you two get on those oars and row toward the stern of the ship."

"The what?"

"The end of the ship, stupid. That way." The man pointed.

A flush warmed the back of Marcus's neck and he swallowed hard. He and Samantha both edged to the sides of the lifeboat where the oars were locked into position. Placing their hands on them, they tried to move in unison.

Not used to rowing a boat, there were several false starts, accompanied by snarled directions from the MM, before they finally got the hang of it and the lifeboat began to move alongside the *Doty*.

As they reached the rear of the ship, a crosswind that had been blocked by its side hit them. It was blowing harder than it had when the twins first went on deck. The waves towered higher as well.

Marcus and Samantha struggled to keep the boat moving.

Marcus rested for a moment. "Mister, I don't know how long we're going to be able to row. We must be coming out of the sucker hole and the storm's getting ready to start again. Where do you want us to go?"

"Shut up and keep rowing kid. You don't have to go any farther than the *Olive Jeanette*. I'm getting off there."

"What about us?" Samantha's question cut into the wind.

The man shrugged. "What about you? You and your brother can keep rowing. You're bound to reach land…sometime."

"You can't do that." Marcus had to raise his voice in protest above the noise the wind and waves were making. He tried to pull harder on the oar. It resisted.

"Sure I can." The man pointed at his waistband. "I've got the knife, remember?"

Marcus and Samantha exchanged glances. They realized the man couldn't care less if they lived or not. They'd find no help from him and there was no chance of rescue.

A four-foot wave slapped the side of the boat and drenched the three of them.

Samantha hissed at Marcus to get his attention.

"What?"

"We've got to do something. The current's carrying us farther and farther from the *Doty*."

"At least we're heading in the right direction for

the *Olive Jeanette*. Maybe they can help us."

The MM leaned forward, waved the knife and pointed it at them. "No talking or somebody gets hurt."

They looked at each other. Thank goodness for twin communication. Marcus knew he and Sami were on the same page. They had to do something fast if they were going to avoid being left in the boat to drown when the storm increased again.

"Take off the life preserver." Marcus spoke out of the corner of his mouth so Samantha could hear but not the MM.

"Huh?"

"Take off the life preserver. I have an idea."

Samantha raised her eyebrows, but started fumbling with the cork circle.

"What are you doing?" The MM's question cut into Marcus's focus on Sami.

She gave the man a glare. "I can't row with this thing on. I'm taking it off."

He shrugged. "Your choice. Make it fast and get back on the oar."

Samantha used both hands to take off the life preserver. She deposited it on the bottom of the lifeboat between her and Marcus.

She again grasped the oar, pulled backward, and whispered. "Now what?"

"The next big wave, grab the preserver ring and jump over the side."

Samantha bit her lip. "You jumping, too?"

"Right behind you."

A couple of pulls on the oars and Marcus spotted

a huge swell of the water building into a blockbuster of a wave. "Get ready."

She gave one frightened glance at the giant wave, reached beside her and grasped one side of the life preserver.

"Watch out!" The MM's shout came as a seven-foot wave suddenly appeared, white foam cresting the top.

"Now!" Marcus shouted and jumped. He saw Samantha leap off the other side of the boat at the same time.

Down.

He could feel himself going deeper and deeper. He struggled not to breathe, fought to rise.

As his lungs neared the bursting point, his head popped above the surface. Treading water, he looked for his sister. The lifeboat had moved several yards past him. He could see the MM making frantic jabs with an oar. But no Samantha.

He turned in the other direction. Relief flooded him as he saw his sister, hanging onto the life preserver, heading toward him. He could tell she was having a hard time fighting the current. Marcus moved toward her at an angle so he could intercept.

After what seemed like hours, but could only be minutes, he reached for the other side of the life preserver.

"Mind if I hitch a ride?" He threw a grin in her direction. "You okay?"

"M...Marko. Thank you, Jesus."

Samantha's grateful words warmed Marcus's heart. Sometimes he wondered if his sibling really cared for him. It was nice to know she did, especially under these crazy circumstances.

They treaded water, caught their respective breaths. The now fast-moving current swept them along within any effort on their part.

In the distance to one side, Marcus could see the lifeboat, seemingly deserted now, spinning in slow circles.

"Marcus, what are we going to do?"

"Pray…and see how God gets us out of this before we freeze…or drown."

CHAPTER 16

The twins clung to the cork circle as the current swept them closer and closer to the bow of the *Olive Jeanette*. The waves had increased in size and the wind blew stronger than ever.

"As soon as we get close to the side of the *Jeanette*, Sami, yell and wave. Hopefully somebody will hear and see us."

"Ri-ight."

Marcus could hear Samantha's teeth chatter as she spoke. He could sympathize. He was so cold his legs and feet were almost numb. They had to be rescued soon or they'd both be too stiff to hold onto the life preserver.

"Kick." Marcus moved his feet as hard and fast as he could. He knew his sister would do the same. They moved even faster toward the schooner as it rapidly approached them.

A couple of minutes later, they drew opposite the *Jeanette*.

"Look," gasped Samantha. "Sailors looking our way. Shout, Marko, shout."

"Right."

They yelled as loud as they could and waved one hand above their heads. They continued to shout and wave as the current swept them fast alongside the ship.

On board, Marcus could see sailors running along the deck, keeping parallel with him and Samantha. One man held a big life preserver with a rope attached. Moving fast, he sped down the deck and got ahead of the twins' position in the water.

Raising the circle above his head, the man flung it into the water. It landed a few feet in front of them. Immediately the current caught it and it began to move away, tantalizing as it floated.

"Kick, Sami, kick. Catch the preserver."

"I *am* kicking."

Marcus could tell from Samantha's tone she was exerting herself as much as possible to stroke her way toward rescue. He did the same.

In a couple more minutes, they had reached their means of escape from the relentless water.

They grasped the huge circle of cork and clasped it with their free hands.

"Put both hands on the big one." Marcus demonstrated as he grabbed the new preserver with his other hand. Samantha followed suit. "I'll try to hold it steady. You duck under and get inside, then me."

"Don't let go, Marko."

"I won't. Go." Marcus clung tighter as his sister's head bobbed under the rim of the preserver and surfaced inside.

Sliding his arm around the circle, Marcus slid underneath and came up next to his sister. He looked up. The sailor who'd thrown the preserver made a

EYE OF THE STORM: The First Token

congratulations motion with his arms. He shouted something, but the noise of wind and waves drowned out his words.

"Hang on, Sami."

"Hands so cold...hurts...." Samantha's voice sounded thin and reedy.

"Don't let go." Before Marcus could say any more he saw a lifeboat moving toward them manned by two sailors rowing hard. A third stood at the front of the boat.

In a short time, Marcus and Samantha found themselves in the lifeboat and were transferred quickly on board the *Olive Jeanette*.

"Let's get you kids below and into some dry clothes." One of the sailors who'd rowed the boat placed a hand behind their backs and gave them gentle shoves forward. "Our cook, Miss Browne, can help your sister change."

As they made their way below deck, Marcus and Samantha gave each other a 'twin look.' Marcus knew they were both grateful to the Lord for saving them from the Mystery Man, the wind and waves. Now they needed God to show them how to get from the *Olive Jeanette* to their home. It would, indeed, be a God-sized task.

# # # #

Half an hour later, Marcus and Samantha, in borrowed, but dry, sailor's clothing, sat at a table in the *Jeanette's* version of a dining salon. Full plates of savory food were placed in front of them, while the ship's cook chatted away. "You kids were certainly fortunate some of our crew spotted you in the water. Otherwise you'd have drowned. There isn't any land for miles. How did you get out there, anyway?"

The twins looked at each other. How could they explain the whole scenario without getting into awkward territory?

"We, ah, probably need to tell the captain, first, Miss Browne." Marcus used his politest voice.

"Oh, right. That's okay. We're one big family on board the *Jeanette*. He'll tell the rest of us. God certainly had his eye on you kids though."

"For sure." Samantha's murmur was so soft Marcus almost missed it.

He took a bite and chewed. "It's awfully good food, Miss Browne. You're a first-rate cook."

Frances Browne grinned. "Thank you, Marcus. I've been cooking on the *Jeanette* for three years and up and down these lakes for ten years in all."

"It's definitely yummy," added Samantha. "We missed lunch, what with all the excitement."

"Well, enjoy it while you can." Miss Browne's face took on a worried expression. "If the storm continues any worse, none of us may have much time to eat for the next few hours or days."

"Days?" The twins chorused the question.

Marcus gulped. "You mean the storm could go on for days?"

Miss Browne nodded. "Sure. These northeasters, or gales, or whatever you want to call them, are ferocious and it's often a long time before they blow themselves out."

Marcus and Samantha exchanged a glance. How much longer would it be before they could try to figure out a way to get home...back to their own time?

"If you kids have eaten all you want, I'll take these dishes to the galley and wash them up." Miss Browne broke into their silent communication. "Your own clothes ought to be dry by now. I put them near the oven after you changed." She smiled. "Although I have to say, you look like real sailors in those outfits."

They looked down at their attire. Both had received clothing from some of the crew...mostly things that were too big. But with sleeves and pant legs rolled up, at least they were dry and warm.

"Thank you." Marcus directed his appreciation toward the cook. "Should we change to our own clothes now?"

"Fine." Miss Brown gathered their used plates and utensils. "You can use the same cabins as before."

She walked to the galley, returned in a couple of minutes, clothing slung over one arm. "Looks like even those heavy jackets got dry. When you've finished, the captain will want to talk to you."

"Yes, ma'am." Marcus's mind began to calculate exactly what and how much they could tell the captain to satisfy him and yet buy them some time to try to find a way home.

It wasn't a challenge he looked forward to.

CHAPTER 17

A short time later, Marcus and Samantha stood on the bridge with the commander of the *Olive Jeanette*.

A man with a kind face introduced himself as Captain David Cadotte. He proceeded to divide his attention between questioning them and watching the sky turn darker and darker.

"I'm sure you kids meant no harm when you took the lifeboat," he said. "But it was a foolish, dangerous thing to do. You could have caused my men harm in trying to rescue you. Or you could have drowned."

The twins exchanged a look. If he only knew.

"I really need to pay attention to this weather that's coming in, so let me talk with you some more, perhaps at the evening meal."

"But, sir." Marcus didn't know what he was going to say, but knew he had to mention the Mystery Man and the bomb. "We should tell you about what's happened."

The captain smiled. "I appreciate that, son, but I'm afraid we've got a real problem with the weather about to hit. I'll talk to you later."

"But...."

"Later, son." The captain's voice was full of authority. " In the meantime, stay out of harm's way.

If the wind gets any worse, and in my experience, it will, you need to stay below decks. We've got more snow and sleet on the way, too."

"Yes, sir." Marcus made a special effort to sound pleasant. The captain needed to know about the bomb, but how could he make him listen when his attention was focused elsewhere? He could tell the captain was concerned about their well-being, but needed to concentrate on sailing the *Jeanette* and preparing for foul weather. "We'll go below now."

"See that you do." Cadotte gestured toward the door. "Can you make it along the deck to the staircase?"

"We can." Samantha spoke for them. She half-turned toward the exit. "C'mon, Marko. Let's head to the cabin."

Without further discussion, the two left the shelter of the bridge. As they walked outside, a fresh gust of wind slammed into them. Icy pellets stung their skin.

"Ouch." Marcus brushed at his face. "Let's get below deck, Sami. This stuff hurts."

Hurrying, yet careful of their footing, they made their way along the deck to an entrance that should lead them below. As the heavy door swung shut behind them, they paused and brushed a snowy, slushy mix from their clothes and themselves.

"Wow, it's getting bad out there again." Samantha sounded worried.

Marcus could understand. He wasn't excited about going through another round of the storm, either.

"Let's get to the cabins. You want to come to

mine?" Marcus headed down the corridor, threw the question over his shoulder.

"Sure." Samantha followed close behind.

When they arrived at Marcus's cabin, the twins went inside and sat on a couple of the bunks attached to the walls of the small room.

For a minute they simply sat in silence, then Samantha heaved a sigh. "This is getting harder and harder, Marko. We're either going to have to tell the captain more about how we got here, and the Mystery Man, or start telling some huge lies."

"We can't do that," said Marcus. "I tried to talk to the captain, but you heard how he cut me off. I wish I could..." he noticed the frown forming on his sister's face, "I wish *we* could figure out a way to get off these ships and get home. I'm afraid if we're gone much longer, Mom and Dad are going to panic and call the police or something. They have to wonder where we are. We've been gone more than a whole day."

Samantha twisted a lock of her hair. "Do you suppose we've been absent in our time the same amount of time we've been here? Or when we return, will it only be a short time and our folks will never know?"

"Hmmm. Good questions. I wish we could talk to Great-Uncle Henry," said Marcus. "He's the only one with the answers."

"Yeah." Samantha's gloomy voice matched her expression.

Marcus absentmindedly stuck his hand in his pocket. His fingers encountered the red stone he'd placed there earlier. Pulling it out, he rubbed it.

Amazing how soothing such a motion could be.

"So any ideas?" Samantha's question broke into his zoned out state.

"Huh?" He smoothed the stone, turned it over and over in his hand. He shook his head. "Nothing. How about you?"

"Nope. Zero. Nada. Zip."

Marcus sighed. "I guess we'll have to wait and see what else takes place. We've prayed. I don't know what else to do."

"Neither do I." Samantha stood. "Let's go visit Miss Browne. She seemed nice. Maybe we could help her fix dinner or something."

"Oh, whee! My favorite thing...peeling potatoes."

"Hush. You don't even know if they're going to have potatoes." Samantha swatted at his shoulder. "Come on. It's better than sitting here worrying."

Marcus rose. "Okay. Lead the way, Chef."

She wrinkled her nose at him, walked out the door.

Marcus followed, shoved the red stone back in his pocket. Handling something from their own time hadn't made him feel any better. In fact, it had caused what was likely an attack of homesickness. One causing his stomach to lurch from time to time. Missing home was bad, but he also had the weirdest feeling deep inside they hadn't seen the worst of their adventure yet.

What on earth would be next?

# # # #

When the twins reached the galley they found Miss Browne, beads of sweat dotting her face, as she darted back and forth, seeming to be in two places at once.

For a moment, they stood, watched in near awe. How could one woman do so many things all at the same time?

Samantha cleared her throat. "Uh, Miss Browne, could we help you fix some food or something?"

Frances Browne paused. She smiled. "Volunteers? How wonderful. Do either of you know how to peel potatoes?"

"Told you." Marcus made sure his mutter could only be heard by his sister. He gave a huge sigh. "Yes, ma'am. We both do."

Miss Browne studied him for a moment, grinned. "Too bad we aren't having potatoes, then." She chuckled, shook her head. "If you could see the look on your face."

Marcus directed a weak smile at her. "So what can we do to help?"

Without wasting further time, the cook issued a stream of orders. The twins soon found themselves scurrying between the galley and the dining salon carrying dishes, utensils, trays. A huge bowl of salad was placed on the serving window where the sailors could help themselves.

"We need to use up these fresh vegetables," said Miss Browne. She frowned. "If the storm doesn't move on or blow itself out soon, we may be caught here for days. They won't last too long if that's the situation."

D.A. FEATHERLING

Marcus and Samantha exchanged a look. He cleared his throat. "You mean we could be storm-tossed for a long time?"

The cook shrugged. "It happens occasionally. I don't remember a gale this bad in, oh, five or six years."

"But we'll be safe on the *Jeanette*, right?" Marcus couldn't help his anxiety.

"The ship has weathered many a blow," she said. "Captain Cadotte is a first-rate sailor, and as long as we're in tow with the *Doty*, we should be safe. I do wish *Doty's* Captain Smith hadn't decided to leave yesterday since the storm warning signals were out in port." She shook her head. "Ah, well, he's a daring man and I guess he didn't see any danger."

Marcus sucked in a breath. The *Doty*. They had forgotten the Mystery Man and his threat of a bomb planted on the *Doty*.

"Sami." He grabbed his sister by the arm. "We've got to go tell the Captain about the..." he gave a nervous glance at Miss Browne who stood a short distance away. "The MM. Remember? He said he'd put a...." he lowered his voice even more. "A bomb on board and he'd set the timer. We've got to warn the *Doty*. This time I'll make the captain listen."

Samantha's mouth gaped open. A gasp escaped from her lips. "Oh, my goodness. We did forget. How could we?"

"We need to see if we can catch the *Jeanette's* captain. Now." He turned toward the cook. "Miss Browne, how long until dinner?"

"About half an hour. We usually eat at five o'clock

so I have time to clean up before it gets too late."

"We need to talk to the captain." Marcus dropped the handful of napkins he clutched on the nearest table. "We'll come help some more in a little while."

"I doubt you'll be able to walk on the deck to get to the bridge," she said. "The storm was getting worse, last I heard. Don't know if you can talk to him now. You may have to wait for dinner."

"We have to try." Marcus turned toward his twin. "You stay here, Sami. I'll try to make it and talk to him."

"Nope. We'll both go."

He could tell from the stubborn look on Samantha's face no amount of arguing would make her change her mind. "Fine. Let's do it."

They headed for the corridor leading to the nearest staircase.

CHAPTER 18

When they reached the outer door, the twins tried to open it. It didn't budge.

"Pull harder, Sami, we've got to get to the captain so he can signal the *Doty*. The bomb could go off anytime."

"I know. I'm trying."

They managed to crack the door a bit. Marcus slid his fingers into the slight opening and strained. Exerting all their strength, the heavy door finally moved inward enough for them to slip through.

"Oh, my." Samantha's gasp could barely be heard over the noise of the wind. More sleet and snow stung their faces and hands. The icy wind seemed to cut through their clothing and encase them in coldness.

Marcus looked at the sea. Waves higher than anything he'd ever seen rose almost to height of the sides of the ship, then crashed back into the water. "I don't know, Sami. Those waves are six or seven feet tall. If one of them hits us, we're gone. They're splashing water across the deck, too."

"I know, Marko. But if we don't get the captain to warn the *Doty*, we may have contributed to the deaths of seventeen men."

He gave one brief nod. "Okay. Hold hands, and

let's grab anything on deck we can latch onto to help us get to the bridge. We've got to hurry between waves."

"It's so far away."

"We've gotta do it, Sami. God, help us to make it to the bridge safely."

"Amen," said Samantha. "Okay. Let's go."

Clasping hands, the two began the journey forward, Samantha walking closest to the cargo holds. The gale snatched their breath from them. Snow and sleet pelted their bodies, drenching their clothing once again.

Struggling from deck object to deck object, they slowly made their way toward the bridge.

"Almost there," Marcus yelled. He squeezed his sister's hand.

Samantha's face registered comprehension, but she didn't try to yell over the wind.

A few more minutes and the two reached the entrance to the bridge. Pushing the door together, they almost tumbled inside the room.

"What in the world...." Captain Cadotte's voice held disbelief with a touch of anger. "Why are you kids out in the storm? You could have been swept away."

"Yessir." Marcus tried to keep his teeth from chattering. "We realize it was dangerous, but, Captain, the *Doty* is in danger and you have to warn them."

The captain looked at them in disbelief. "Danger for the *Doty*? This storm is dangerous for every vessel on Lake Michigan. Besides, as big and heavy as the ship is, they're in a better position to survive the gale than we are."

"Not if a bomb goes off." Marcus tried to sound grown up.

"A bomb? What are you talking about?" Cadotte stared at Marcus and Samantha.

"I tried to tell you before. We weren't in the lifeboat where your men rescued us because we wanted to be," said Marcus. "We were held at knifepoint by a man on the *Doty* who said he'd planted a bomb. It could go off anytime."

"Explain." The captain's grim expression showed he was giving his full attention to the twins.

The two, almost talking over each other at times, told about the Mystery Man, his threats, and the danger to the *Doty*.

When they finished, the captain shook his head. "This is hard to believe." He gave them a suspicious look. "Are you sure you two aren't telling me some story because I wouldn't listen to you earlier?"

Marcus frowned. "Do you think we'd be stupid enough to take out a lifeboat by ourselves in the middle of the storm by choice? It's true all right. And there probably isn't much time before the bomb goes off."

Samantha interrupted. "Isn't there some way you can warn the *Doty*?"

Cadotte considered, finally shook his head. "I don't see how. We can't use signal flags. They wouldn't be seen in this wind, and if we tried to launch a lifeboat, it wouldn't last a minute in the waves. They're sometimes up to twenty feet now.

Plus the snow and sleet are making visibility almost zero. We're only a little way past Milwaukee, but there won't be any help from another ship. I don't know of anything we can do."

Concern etched itself on all three faces.

"So we do nothing." Sorrow drenched Marcus's heart.

The captain took a deep breath. "I can't think of...."

He was interrupted by a loud twang. A noise so powerful it could be heard above the storm. The *Jeanette* gave a mighty lurch, swung to one side. The captain's hands whirled the wheel to correct the ship back to its original course.

"What was that?" Marcus shouted.

Cadotte appeared grim. "I'm afraid we're in more trouble than from the storm. Our towline to the *Doty* just snapped. We're on our own at the mercy of the storm."

Marcus and Samantha exchanged a horrified look.

Marcus managed to take a deep breath. "Could it...could the bomb have gone off and what we heard was the explosion?"

The captain shook his head. "No, it was the towline snapping. It happens sometimes in a severe storm. And this is one of the worst I've ever seen. You kids must get below deck...now. I need to focus on what's happening and not be worried about your safety here on the bridge.

"The weather is only going to get more intense before it gets better. I'd like to send one of the crew to help you below, but I need every sailor aboard to try to get some sails up to keep us from sinking right away."

"We'll go help Miss Browne," offered Samantha.

"Fine. Just get off the deck. Go."

"We'll pray, too," said Marcus.

The captain's expression softened. "That's our only hope. You kids pray and the crew will too. It's going to be strictly in God's hands whether we make it back to harbor or not. Be careful."

Marcus and Samantha looked at each other, headed for the door. They'd better return to the galley. If they could.

The wind blew the twins sideways as they crept along the deck, holding onto anything permanently attached to the ship.

"Marko, I don't think we can make it." Samantha's voice rang in his left ear.

"We have to. Let's get down, Sami. Make ourselves smaller. We can crawl if we need to. It's not much further to a staircase door."

"I'll try."

The two lowered themselves to the deck. Continuing to grasp immovable objects, they crawl-walked to the nearest door leading below.

Grasping the doorknob in one hand, Marcus held the other out to his sister. "C'mon, Sami. Help me with the door."

They tugged as hard as they could, but it wasn't until the wind died for a few precious seconds, that they were able to turn the knob and slip inside to the staircase. The door slammed shut behind them as the next wind gust hit it.

"Whew." Marcus swiped water from his head. "I wasn't sure we were going to make it."

Samantha wiped her face. "Me either. What are we going to do, Marcus? There's no way to warn the *Doty*. The bomb is going to go off and the *Doty* is going to sink."

His eyes teared. "Yeah, and all those people...." He sniffed. "There's nothing we can do. The storm is in charge of everything."

"Not really."

Samantha's quiet statement took him by surprise. "What do you mean?"

"I mean God's in control of it all. The outcome is in his hands." Samantha twisted a lock of her hair. "We have to hope and pray the *Doty*...and the *Jeanette*...don't sink in the storm."

Marcus thought for a moment. "Yeah, we've done all we can. But I hate for the Mystery Man to get away with a crime, if he does."

Samantha squeezed his shoulder. "Maybe the bomb will get wet from all the water and snow. Maybe it won't go off."

"True." Marcus felt the knot in his stomach begin to dissolve. "Our Mystery Man may not know much about making bombs. He could have messed up."

"I wonder where he is now." Samantha's expression was troubled.

"Dunno. But he's an adult, and he could probably row the lifeboat by himself to shore or wherever the current drifted him."

"Right." Samantha started down the staircase. "Come on. Let's get back to the galley. Miss Browne

116

may need our help."

The twins threaded their way through the corridors until they reached the dining salon.

Walking inside, they saw the cook had finished setting out stacks of bowls near the stove where she could fill them when the crew arrived.

"Miss Browne?" Marcus called. "We're back. Can we do anything?"

The cook stuck her head out the galley door. "Help me make sandwiches. I was going to cook a meal, but the ship is moving up and down so much from the wind and waves, I can't keep the pans on the stove. I've got the coffeepot rigged where it's okay for now…but if the storm keeps up, I don't know how I'm going to serve any meals."

"We'll help," said Marcus. "Show us what to do."

"Over here, then." Miss Browne gestured to a long table at one side. "You can put out the bread and your sister can put some slices of meat and cheese on it. I'll finish making coffee."

A sudden jolt caused the three of them to almost lose their balance. Samantha gave a shriek; Miss Browne clutched a nearby doorway.

They all steadied themselves.

Marcus looked at her. "What was that?"

"I suspect we got washed over by a wave. With twenty to thirty foot waves out there, everything on deck could be washed overboard. Including the crew."

Marcus and Samantha gazed at her, speechless.

The cook shook herself. "Let's get busy. If this keeps up, it may be our last chance to fix any food."

She turned and headed toward her work station, muttering to herself. "It may be our last chance for anything."

CHAPTER 19

As Marcus put the final slice of bread on top of the fillings Samantha had added, a seaman rushed into the dining salon.

"Miss Frances."

Miss Browne jerked around. "What is it, Mr. Combs?"

"Waves are hitting thirty-five feet high and the wind is at sixty miles an hour. Water is smashing over the deck and it's started leaking below. Stay in the galley."

She shuddered. "Understood."

Combs's face assumed a grim expression. "Captain's determined to stay on the bridge to keep up with where we're heading as much as possible now the towline snapped."

"Snapped." She took a deep breath. Her pale skin flushed along the cheekbones. "What can I do to help?"

"Keep the coffee coming as long as you can. And stay alert. You're gonna have a lot of water in here before long."

She nodded. "We'll do our best, Mr. Combs. Do you want me to bring up the coffee when it's done?"

"You can try. If you can't make it one of the men

will come down and get it. If you have anything easy to eat, you might send it, too. We're going to need our strength to keep the *Jeanette* afloat."

Miss Browne squared her shoulders. "I'll do my part. Coffee should be ready in ten minutes and we've got sandwiches made."

Combs glanced at the array of food lined up on the table. "Good. I'll have someone come get it. Can you wrap it in something to try to keep it dry?"

"I've got some cloths we can use." The cook's words were brisk.

Without a further word Combs wheeled and left the galley.

The twins and the cook stared at each other. Miss Browne shook herself. "You heard him, kids. We have to be prepared. Get those coffee cups ready. Use the metal ones. You'll need six."

"Six?" croaked Marcus. His dry throat made normal speech impossible.

"That's how many crew members there are. Oh, and here...." She walked over to a cabinet on one wall, opened the door, and pulled out three life preservers. "Put these on. If the water gets too high in here we may need them."

Marcus and Samantha shared a look, gulped, took the items she handed them.

"Well," Marcus tried to inject a note of bravery. "At least we each get our own life jacket this time."

Samantha cracked a tiny smile. "Always something to be grateful for."

Without further conversation, the twins donned the preservers, then began collecting coffee cups and wrapping sandwiches.

Miss Browne put everything into a heavy basket, along with the steaming coffeepot. "Ready. Whenever one of the seamen comes, he can take the basket. Hope they'll bring the pot back. I only have one other one."

"Should we go ahead and make another pot of coffee?" asked Samantha.

The cook cocked her head to one side, considered. "Wouldn't hurt. We can get the water and the grounds into it, anyway."

"Look." Marcus pointed toward the galley door leading to the dining salon.

All three of them watched as a thin line of water snaked its way under the door toward where they stood.

Samantha gulped. "I guess we're about to start wading."

They watched in dismay as the river of icy water spread out, crept around the soles of their shoes, and toward the far wall of the galley.

"Don't just stand there," said Miss Browne. "If it's getting this bad below deck, we'd better see what it looks like in the other room, too." She gestured toward the dining salon. "The crew will have to come through there to get to us."

Marcus held his breath as the cook sloshed her way to the door, pulled it open. The level of the water in the galley instantly rose a few inches. Water now lapped at the top of his shoes.

"It's rising pretty fast, isn't it?" He tried to keep his voice from squeaking.

"Thank goodness we've got the life preservers." Samantha sounded strained.

The three stood and stared as the water continued to swirl around their feet.

The sound of the outer door of the dining salon jerked them back to reality. One of the seamen stood there, a life preserver around his middle. His beard glistened with water, his clothing soaked and clinging to him.

"Anybody got some coffee for a cold crew?" His cheerful voice penetrated their numbness.

"Just a minute, Mr. Mills." Miss Browne went back into the galley, returned carrying the heavy basket. "There's coffee and sandwiches. You be sure I get the pot back."

The seaman's swift grin brought a cheerful note into the atmosphere. "I'll do it, Miss Frances."

"What's going on topside?"

The cook's question wiped away the man's smile. "It's bad, ma'am. The captain's worried about losing sails or the rudder. Without those, we won't be able to steer at all."

"Hope they stay intact, then."

Mills nodded. "Yes'm. I'd better go. The others'll be wanting something hot to drink."

The seaman waded to the door and exited the salon.

The three left behind watched him until he disappeared from sight. Miss Browne heaved a sigh.

"Now what?" asked Marcus. "What do we do now?"

"Praying is a good idea," said Samantha. "Do you

want to join us, Miss Browne?"

The three seated themselves at one of the dining tables and bowed their heads.

# # # #

The next few hours went by in blurred fashion. Men came and went, taking a filled coffeepot and leaving an empty one. Miss Browne and the twins kept the stove going, with a fresh pot ready each time.

At another offer of sandwiches, the seaman who'd come to get the coffee shook his head. "No time to eat, Miss Frances. We've got all we can do to try to keep the sails up. They're starting to shred from the wind."

"What's our condition?" The cook's question brought a solemn look to the man's face.

He shook his head. "We're barely holding on. Don't know how long we can keep afloat, though. If we get much more damage...." He frowned. "I've got to get back. Thanks for the coffee."

"Could we go to our cabins and rest?" Samantha's query brought Miss Frances's attention to the girl.

"I wish you could, dearie," she said. "But the men don't seem to think it's safe. Why don't you try sitting at one of the tables and putting your head down on your arms? Maybe you can get a little sleep."

Marcus and Samantha exchanged glances, sighed, settled themselves next to each other on a bench. The cold water lapped above their ankles.

They laid their heads on their crossed arms, faces toward each other.

"Marko," whispered Samantha. "What do you

think's going to happen to us?"

He shook his head. "I don't have a clue, Sami. We're in a dangerous situation and I can't figure how we're going to get out of it."

She sniffed. "Maybe we won't."

Marcus could tell she was near tears. He reached over and squeezed her arm. "Don't give up, Sis. There's bound to be a way to get off the ship and back home."

"Yes, but how?" Samantha's voice assumed the sound of a wail. "I wish we'd never heard of Great-Uncle Henry and his crazy inventions. If it weren't for him, we wouldn't be here."

Marcus couldn't keep quiet. "True. But we both wanted an adventure, now didn't we?" He nudged her. "Be honest."

A reluctant grin creased her lips. "I guess. But I didn't expect it to be like this."

Marcus regarded her with a sober look. "I know. I guess you can't choose how an adventure plays out...you have to go where it leads."

Samantha lifted one foot from the floor and shook it. Water drops flew in all directions. "I would never have expected to get so soggy or be so cold."

"Same here." Marcus reached in his pocket and fingered the red stone he'd brought from home. He stayed quiet for a minute. "Sami, do you suppose Mom and Dad have missed us and are worried about where we are?"

She shrugged, bit her lower lip. "I don't know. Maybe they don't know we're gone. We've got to get home soon, Marko. We've got to. We can't go down with the ship over a hundred years in the past. Nobody would ever know what happened to us."

They stared at each other. Both of them sighed at the same time.

"Well," Marcus tried to inject a note of hope. "Maybe the storm will be over soon and...."

Suddenly the ship shifted, tilted onto its side. Objects not attached to something solid flew through the air or slid over into the water.

Samantha screamed. "What's going on?" Her voice shook with fear.

The outside door to the salon burst open. One of the seamen came through the doorway, tried to clutch the framework with one hand. The other hand held the basket containing the coffeepot and cups.

The man slid to a stop, face pale. "The rudder chains are broken. Just when we were in sight of Racine Harbor. Now we've turned broadside to the waves. The *Jeanette* is like a cigar box being crushed under the iron wheels of a wagon."

Frances Browne gave an agonized cry. "What about the others?"

"All safe for now," the man replied. "The cap'n's lashed himself to the wheel so he won't get washed away. The rest of us are tying ourselves to anything that hasn't gone overboard. But with the sea so high, don't know how long the *Jeanette* can last."

"What should we do?" The question burst from Marcus's throat without conscious thought.

"Best stay where you are," said the seaman. "We've lost most of the sails, the lifeboat's gone and with the rudder not working, we're at the mercy of the wind and the waves."

"And God's mercy." Samantha's steady voice broke into the quiet following the man's comment.

They all looked at each other. Everyone glanced down as though ashamed of their lack of faith.

"Aye," said the seaman. "It'll be in God's hand, all right. If you can keep making us coffee through the night, Miss Frances, it'll be a lifesaver."

"I don't know what shape the stove is in," she said, "but I'll check it out and make more somehow."

The seaman thrust the basket into her hands. "I'd best go. The others need my help. The engine's broken, too, and the steam pump isn't working. We're going to be manning the hand pumps for quite a while."

He staggered out the door, lurching as the ship heaved like an untamed bucking horse trying to throw a rider.

Miss Frances held her head high. "Come on, then, you two. We've got a job to do. The men need coffee to keep going...so we'll give them coffee. You can help."

Marcus and Samantha exchanged glances, followed the cook toward the galley. Water to their knees swirled around them. How long before it got too high for them to keep their footing? What would happen then?

CHAPTER 20

"What day is it?" Marcus rubbed sleep from his eyes, raised his head from resting on his forearms draped across the table. He frowned. Water lapped around his hips, almost to his waist.

Frances Browne jerked awake. She stretched, yawned. "Can't believe we actually slept." She studied Samantha who still had her head pillowed on her arms. "Your sister must be able to sleep through anything."

Marcus couldn't stifle a grin. "She's a sound sleeper, all right."

"I heard that," Samantha mumbled. She yawned and squinted at the others. "What time is it?"

Miss Browne considered. "It must be Wednesday, sometime in the afternoon. Seaman McQuarry brought the coffeepot back last night and said the engine broke.

"All the sailors are manning the hand pump ever since to try to keep the ship afloat. The men have been working all night and since daylight this morning. But it's dangerous. Sometimes the waves fall on them and completely submerge them. They have to hold on to the iron braces for dear life to keep from being swept overboard."

She climbed from the bench and stretched. "I'd better make more coffee."

"Should we make some sandwiches?" Samantha also stood, flexed her shoulders.

"Good idea," said Miss Browne. "They haven't eaten anything since yesterday. Don't want to take time away from the pumping, but they've got to have some fuel or they won't have the energy to continue. You kids make a dozen cheese sandwiches. Enough for the men and captain, and us, to each have one. I doubt if they'll take long to eat. They'll have to hold the food in one hand and work the pump with the other."

Marcus joined his sister. "Right. We'll take care of it."

He and Samantha headed for the galley, pulled themselves along from table to table to doorway. The water pulled against them, tiring them every time they moved. He shook his head. It looked weird with everything sideways from where it should be. Oh, well. As long as the water didn't rise any more.

# # # #

Marcus and Samantha worked more than they ever had the rest of the day and during the night that followed to help keep the crew fed.

The storm raged all night harder than ever. The water in the galley reached the stove and put the fire out. The carpet pulled loose from the floor of the dining salon and the oil cloth was torn off the floor of the galley by the force of the flood.

"We can't have that." Miss Browne frowned as she surveyed the stove. "Here, kids, help me. We're going to straighten it enough so I can make coffee."

The three of them grabbed different sides of the stove. Heaving with all their might, they managed to lean the stove in a semi-upright position.

"It's the best we can do," puffed Marcus. His breath came in short gasps.

"Good enough," declared the cook. "I'll fasten myself to a stanchion to rebuild the fire and get a pot of coffee going. You kids go back in the salon, though. If the water keeps rising and the stove detaches, I don't want either of you getting hurt."

They backed away, headed for the other room.

"Come on," said Samantha. "Maybe we can perch on top of the tables to get out of the water a while. I'm beginning to feel as wrinkled as a prune."

"We probably resemble prunes," teased Marcus.

Horror crossed Samantha's face. "Do I have wrinkles?" She pushed at the skin on her cheeks, first one direction then another.

Marcus snorted. "Joking, Sami. Joking."

"Hmmph. Very funny." She splashed through the waist-high water into the salon. "Here, we can sit on this table."

The side edge of the table barely showed above the water level. At least it would give them a brief rest from being soggy.

They had barely climbed onto the table when a loud clank came from the galley.

"You okay, Miss Browne?" Marcus yelled loud enough for the cook to hear.

"I'm all right," came her reply. "Since we're listing to the side, the stove isn't straight since it's bolted to the floor and I have to hold the pot on it to heat the water for coffee. It's fine."

Marcus gave Samantha a sober look. "You know, Sami, there are a lot of heroes on this ship. Imagine what those poor sailors have gone through the last few days, hand pumping water out of the interior of the boat. They've got to be exhausted. And Miss Browne, keeping them all going with her coffee and sandwiches. She's a heroine, too."

"I know." Samantha slumped as she perched on the table. "I'm so tired it's unreal, and I haven't worked anywhere near as hard."

They fell silent. In a few minutes, Marcus straightened. "Sami, we've got to figure a way to get home. This may be our only chance to have a few minutes alone. The ship is either going to go down soon, or we'll be rescued. Regardless, we need to get off it as quickly as we can."

She nodded. "I know. Any ideas?"

Marcus concentrated as hard as he could on the problem. "Lord, give me some answers." He waited a moment. No ideas came to him. He shook his head. "No. You?"

Samantha shook her head as well. "Nope. Nothing. I guess we're going to have to wait for an opportunity...whatever it is...and take advantage of it when it occurs."

"That's pretty iffy," said Marcus. "But you're right. We'll have to trust God to give us the idea and the timing and go with it."

"Could use some help in here." Miss Browne's voice broke up their discussion.

"Coming." Marcus slid off the tabletop into the water. "C'mon, Sami."

# # # #

Half an hour later, Frances Browne arrayed herself in a raincoat. "I know I look pretty silly," she told the twins. "But it'll help keep the snow and sleet from hitting my skin while I'm on deck."

"Are you sure this is a good idea, Miss Browne?" Marcus hated to see anything harm the brave cook.

"I've got to do it, Marcus. The captain's tied to the wheel, he can't come get coffee, and the others are pumping water out of the *Jeanette* as fast as they can. 'Course more water's coming in about as fast, but they've got to keep on helping us stay afloat." She shook her head. "No, taking the cap'n a cup of my coffee is the least I can do."

A sinking feeling in Marcus's stomach told him it wasn't a great idea, but he couldn't stop the woman.

"We'll pray for you," Samantha said.

Miss Browne nodded. "Good. I'll return as soon as I can. You kids stay away from the stove."

"We will," Marcus assured her. "Be careful."

She grinned, sketched a salute, then walked toward the door, coffee cup cradled against her to keep the liquid from sloshing out.

Marcus and Samantha watched her disappear from sight.

Samantha sighed. "I wish she wouldn't go on

deck. She's so thin she could get blown away in a minute."

"Let's pray now," said Marcus.

The twins bowed their heads and offered their prayers.

They'd barely finished, when Frances Browne waded into the salon.

"What happened?" Marcus could tell from the look on her face the trip hadn't been a success.

"Couldn't get it to the cap'n. A wave hit me when I left the companionway and knocked the coffee out of the cup. I barely held on to the doorway and the cup. Gotta try again."

The twins stood, speechless, as the woman walked toward the galley.

She emerged a few minutes later, clutching another steaming cup. "Be back in a minute."

They watched in awe and admiration as Miss Browne again waded out of the salon and into the corridor.

"That's got to be the bravest thing I've ever seen." Samantha shook her head. "The men wouldn't be able to keep going if it weren't for her taking them coffee."

"Yeah," said Marcus. "She's even been delivering it to the crew as they pump water. Guess heroes come in all sizes and shapes."

"Hope she gets it to the captain," said Samantha. "I don't know how many more trips she can make before she wears out from exhaustion."

"I wish there was something we could do to help." Marcus looked thoughtful. "Any ideas?"

Samantha shook her head. "No. Be available to

make more sandwiches, I guess." She twiddled with a damp lock of hair. "Marko, I'm beginning to wonder if we're ever going to get off the ship. Get home to our own time."

Marcus didn't know how to respond. Deep inside, he wondered the same things himself. He didn't want to discourage his twin, however, therefore he wouldn't echo her concerns. He reached over and gave her an awkward pat on the shoulder. "Don't give up, Sami. God's gonna get us out of here. We have to believe that."

"I'm trying," said Samantha, "but it's hard sitting...or standing...in all this water. I'm so cold I almost can't feel my feet any more. And I'm so waterlogged I feel like sponge in a giant bathtub."

"Except you've got a whole lake to get wet in." Marcus wanted his attempt at humor to help. A quick glance at his sister's face showed a glimmer of amusement. Maybe he could help her keep up her spirits. He tried to think of something else funny to say.

A hiss interrupted his thinking.

They both checked the sideways, watery room. "It's the cats." Their voices blended as they saw the Jeanette's two cats perched on the side of a bookcase floating in the water. The animals sat on the wooden structure as calmly as though on dry land.

"How did they get there?" Marcus wondered out loud. "Look, Sami, they're licking themselves dry."

A huge smile spread across Samantha's face. "Let's go get them." She started moving toward the cats.

"No, wait." Marcus caught her arm. "If you scare them, they might jump off into the water."

"So? They can obviously swim or they wouldn't be in here."

"Doesn't matter," said Marcus. "There aren't too many pieces of furniture for them to sit on. If we scare them off, they could drown. We'd better leave them alone. If they want us to come to them, I imagine they'll meow or something to let us know."

"What if they're hungry?" Samantha's question wasn't unreasonable.

"Let's wait until Miss Browne gets back. She'll know when and how they eat. If they need food, they'd probably let her get close enough to give them something.

"Besides they're used to her and they've never seen us before. They've evidently been out of sight the whole time we've been aboard the *Jeanette*. I don't remember seeing them."

"All right." Samantha moved a few steps closer to Marcus. "But if she doesn't return soon, I'm going to try to help the poor things."

"Doesn't seem like they need much help to me." Marcus watched as one of the cats stopped licking and lay down on the bookcase. "They're drier than we are."

The twins stood there, comforted a little by the ordinary sight of two cats in the middle of the room.

Marcus smirked. "Guess you could call this a 'cat-astrophe,'" he said.

Samantha punched his arm. "Oh, you. No more bad jokes. Let's see what Miss Browne says. She ought to be back soon. She's been gone a really long time."

They looked toward the salon door. Surely the cook would be here shortly.

CHAPTER 21

Sloshing sounds heading their way caused Marcus's heart to skip a beat. Was it Miss Browne? Or some member of the crew with news the cook had been injured or washed overboard?

A minute later, the slight form of Frances Browne waded through the doorway into the salon.

"Miss Browne," Samantha moved through the water and gave the woman a hug. "We were so worried about you."

The cook hugged her back. "Thought I was a goner a time or two, but the good Lord kept me steady. I was able to crawl close enough to the captain to hand him the coffee. Poor man. He looks exhausted. But he's keeping his hands on the wheel and watching for any sign the storm is blowing itself out. He said he thinks it should be over later today."

"I hope so," said Samantha. "I've had enough water to last me the rest of my life."

Miss Browne smiled. "I can understand that. But you know, these storms are the exception, not the rule. I've made many a voyage with the weather as calm as anything. You kids keep praying. We'll get through this yet."

She headed toward the galley. "I'm gonna make

another pot of coffee for the crew. They'll need something hot, too."

Marcus and Samantha watched as she waded through the waist deep water into the galley. Clanging metal soon informed them another pot was on the stove, even if Miss Browne had to hold it in place with a folded cloth while it boiled, as she'd been doing.

"She is one outstanding lady." Marcus had to voice his admiration.

"She certainly is." Samantha shook her head. "I don't think I'd be able to do what she's doing. Let alone be optimistic about our chances of coming through the storm alive."

Marcus stood in the water, hand plunged into his pocket, again fingering the red stone deep inside. "Maybe she's right, Sami. Maybe the storm is about over."

Samantha swallowed hard. "Then we should concentrate on figuring out how to get home."

They both sighed.

"Well," Marcus shook himself as though coming awake. "I don't have any great ideas at the moment. I'm about ready to drape myself over a table and try to take a nap. I've never been so tired."

"I know what you mean." Samantha sounded exhausted.

More coldness crept over Marcus. Looking down he saw the water had risen again. Now it was halfway up his chest. He ground his teeth, hoped they wouldn't chatter. Much more water and they'd all be awash. Miss Browne wasn't much taller than him and

Samantha. If they went underwater, so would she. No, it mustn't happen.

He grinned, then sobered, as he remembered the life preserver she still wore. She'd never taken it off these several days. Maybe he and Samantha should put theirs back on again. They'd removed them yesterday since it was uncomfortable to have the things under their arms. But with the water still rising, perhaps they should get them on.

"Sami." He raised his voice to be sure she could hear above the banging noises going on in the galley. "Come over here."

"What?" Samantha turned and waded in his direction.

"Let's put our life preservers on." Marcus spoke in a quieter tone now she was closer. The galley clatter had ceased for the moment. Miss Browne was probably holding the coffeepot steady on the stove.

Samantha wore a troubled expression. "Do you really think we need to?"

"Look at the water, Sami. It's halfway up my chest. Before long, it could be to my neck. Do you want to take a chance if it rises higher? With the preservers on, at least we can float."

"You're right." Samantha bit her lip. "We need to take all the precautions we can."

They moved toward the pegs on the wall where they'd hung the life preservers. When they reached them, Marcus lifted the devices down. He helped Samantha put on hers, then slid his over his shoulders and under his arms.

"Better test them out," he suggested. He took his

feet off the floor and let his weight rest on the cork circle. His body immediately gained buoyancy and he floated a few inches away. "Mine works." He turned toward Samantha. "Take your feet off the floor, hang on, and see if you float."

"Right." A moment later, she drifted a couple of inches forward. "Seems to work fine."

Marcus swallowed a sigh of relief. If the worst should happen and the water continued to deepen, they had a chance for survival. If only the storm would stop and give the *Jeanette* and her crew a chance to be rescued. No telling where the ship had drifted as battered as it was by the wind and waves.

He sent another prayer heavenward. He would love to be home again. In his own room. No weird game to get involved in. No strange adventures. If only he could figure out how they could get back. He touched his pocket where the game's red stone resided. Right now, the little piece of rock represented home. It was all he had to remember it by.

Marcus bit his lip. Surely, God would get them out of the situation and back to their own time soon.

# # # #

Marcus jerked awake. He leaned against Samantha where they both perched on one of the tabletops. By wedging a broom handle in a crack in the middle of a table, and each hooking an elbow around it, they'd managed to keep themselves from floating away as they sat.

His arms ached from clutching the broom. He

flexed his shoulder. At his tiny movements, Samantha shifted position, then moved more freely.

"Marcus? What's going on?"

"I just woke up. Don't know how long we've been asleep. We'd better check on Miss Browne, see if she needs any help."

They inched around the broom handle and stood. The water still reached mid-chest level.

"Doesn't look like the water's gotten any higher. Guess the crew's pumping is keeping the level down." Marcus couldn't believe the relief he felt.

"Or maybe we weren't asleep very long." Samantha moved slowly toward the galley door. "Miss Browne? Do you need some help?"

No response.

They waded a little faster through the murky water. When they reached the galley doorway, they both peered inside. No sign of Frances Browne.

"Marcus, she's not here. Where do you suppose she's gone?"

"I don't see the coffeepot, Sami. I imagine she's on deck, pouring hot drinks for the crew."

"You're probably right." Samantha sighed. "I feel guilty for letting her do all the work."

"We're only kids," Marcus said. "It's her job and I doubt if she'd let us do much more than we already have. We need to let her do her thing and we'll be available if there's something we can help with."

"Good points." Samantha turned and looked at the flooded salon. "So now what do we do? Practice our swimming strokes? This is scary, Marko, but it's also pretty boring."

"Yep. There's nothing to do but wait until something changes."

As Marcus finished his statement, he heard the sound of sloshing water. A few seconds later, Miss Browne appeared in the dining salon doorway.

"Did you two have a good nap?" She clutched the coffeepot, covered with cloths to keep her hands from being burned.

"We're fine." Marcus studied the pot. "Did you already serve the men coffee?"

She shook her head. "Couldn't get to them. I was close enough to where I could yell at them and one said they'd all lashed themselves to anything that hadn't washed overboard and were waiting out the storm. They told me to get below and stay here until the weather calms. So…here I am."

She bit her lower lip and sighed. "I wanted to help by getting the coffee to them…." Her voice trailed off.

"Come on in," said Marcus. "We were just trying to figure out what to do when you showed up." He tried for a lighter note. "We thought we might practice our swimming. Are you any good at the butterfly stroke?"

The cook snorted with laughter. "Nope. In fact, I can't swim." She patted her life preserver. "It's why I wear this thing."

Marcus and Samantha mouths gaped.

Finally Samantha spoke. "You…can't…swim? And you work on a ship?"

Miss Browne's face tinged pink. "Sounds crazy, doesn't it? But you know, a lot of the crew on ships don't know how."

Marcus couldn't believe his ears. "Wow. That is the wildest thing I've ever heard."

"How about you two?" she asked. "Do you know how to swim?"

"Sure," said Marcus. "We both learned how at the 'Y' a few summers ago."

"The Y? You mean the YMCA? I didn't know they taught swimming?" Miss Browne sounded curious.

The twins looked at each other. Oops. They'd have a hard time answering. Especially since they didn't know what year the Y had added swimming to their curriculum.

"Er...we...ah...." Marcus began, thinking fast. How could he explain more without giving too much information?

As he opened his mouth, a shout reverberated down the corridor.

## CHAPTER 22

"Ahoy, Miss Frances. Storm's over. You and the kids can come out now."

Marcus's heart beat double time. The storm had stopped. They weren't going to drown?

He and Samantha exchanged looks. He could feel his own broad grin and saw the same thing on his sister's face.

"We're saved! Hurray!" Marcus cheered while a mixture of relief and anticipation swept over him.

"Hurray!" Samantha and Miss Browne echoed.

The cook hooked the coffeepot handle over a peg on the wall. A small stream of coffee ejected from the spout. She ignored the spill and held out her hands to the twins.

Joining hands, they did a watery victory dance in the middle of the salon.

"Let's go on deck." Marcus suddenly couldn't wait to get away from water. He'd turn into a fish if he didn't dry out soon.

"Right behind you." Samantha yelled. "Come on, Miss Browne. Let's go see what's happening topside."

The three of them made their way through the corridor to the staircase. As they climbed higher and higher up the stairs, streams of water poured off all of them. The list of the ship, still partially lying on its side, made progress difficult.

When they reached the deck, devastation met them. Shreds of a sail hung from the one remaining mast. The deck was bare except for the few structures that had survived the battering waves.

A watery-looking sun peeked weakly from a clearing sky. Crew members were busy picking up shredded sails and bits of lumber from the deck.

"Where's the Captain?" Miss Browne gave an anxious scan of the almost completely bare deck. "Oh, there he is." She waved. "Captain...Captain Cadotte...are you all right?"

The captain made his way toward them with a relieved smile. "Miss Browne, children, thank God you're safe."

"Thank Him we all are." Miss Browne's husky reply showed the depth of emotion she concealed inside. "Any idea where we are?"

"As best as I can reckon, we're adrift somewhere near Chicago."

"Great," said Marcus. "Somebody should see us soon and come to our rescue, won't they?"

"Right." The captain's reply was emphatic, but weary.

Marcus couldn't believe the man was able to stand after being lashed to the wheel for three days in the middle of a raging storm. "You're a hero, sir."

A faint pink rose in the captain's cheeks. "Just doing my job, son. Just doing my job."

"Still, we thank you, my sister and I, and I know the crew does too, for your efforts to keep us afloat and save us. Thank you, Captain."

The crew gathered around. "Three cheers for the Captain." The seamen, cook, and the twins gave three hearty cheers.

Captain Cadotte stood there, red-faced with embarrassment at the outpouring of emotion. He cleared his throat. "Thanks to all of you for your help. We all played a part in staying alive." He turned toward Frances Browne. "You're a hero, too, Miss Frances. If it hadn't been for your coffee, we'd never have had the strength to keep going. When I think of how you risked your life to bring us a hot drink...well, like I said, you're a hero."

The sailors gave another round of cheers.

"Enough standing around." Captain Cadotte gestured. "We need to see if we can find something to use to signal the next ship that comes our way." He glanced over the deck. "There's one mast still there. Let's run up a signal on it. Hopefully someone will see it and come for us."

Marcus checked his soaked clothing. His shoes squished whenever he moved his feet.

"Let's get over here out of the way, Sami," he said. "Maybe we can dry out a little bit before we're rescued."

Samantha cast a worried look at the choppy waters of the grayish lake. "I don't see anything headed our way. It might be a while."

They moved aside as the crew scattered, searching for any piece of cloth or other material large enough to use as a signal flag.

An hour or so later, the seamen had found one

lone shirt that had escaped being washed overboard. Using rope, they rigged a type of flag and attached it to the single remaining mast.

Since the ship still lay on its side, everyone moved carefully along the deck, grabbing anything solid for a handhold as they went from one place to the next.

"It would be nice to have some dry clothes to change into," said Marcus.

"I imagine the crew thinks so, too," Samantha said. Sympathy drenched her voice. "They've been in those wet clothes for days. And I heard someone say all of their belongings were in the crew's cabin which was swept off the deck."

Marcus fingered his still damp attire. "It's getting a little cool on deck, Sami. Do you want to go below and get out of the wind?"

"And wade through four or more feet of water? I don't think so."

"Oh, right. Well, guess we'll have to wait out a rescue, but I wish they'd hurry."

Samantha looked down the length of the deck. "Look, Marko. One of the seamen has climbed to the front of the ship and is perched on top. Guess he's keeping watch for another vessel."

The twins watched the man scan the horizon. They could see nothing from where they stood, but since the seaman was higher than they, perhaps he'd spot something soon.

A few minutes later, Frances Browne walked toward them. "You two doing okay?" Her face was serene, the life preserver still firmly in place under her arms.

"We're fine," said Samantha. "How about you?"

The cook grinned. "Now I'm out of the water, I'm good. I'll be even better when we get picked up or towed back to port."

A shout sounded from the stern of the ship. "Ahoy! Cap'n! Steamer coming our way."

The crew rushed to the side. So did Marcus, Samantha and Frances Browne. They all squinted at the water, hoping to spot their rescuers.

"There." Marcus pointed. "I can see a little smoke in the sky. It must be the steamer."

"Hurrah!" Miss Browne's enthusiasm washed over them. "Looks like the *City of Grand Rapids*. I recognize the shape. That storm has pushed us back almost to where we started."

Everyone crowded together as they watched the steamer's efforts to draw close. The choppy waters and wind direction appeared to hold the vessel back.

"I don't know if they'll be able to help us." Miss Browne's voice contained a note of despair.

"Here." She extended her hands to the twins who stood one on each side of her. "Let's pray they can get here."

They clutched each other's hands and said a heartfelt prayer.

"I'm going to ask the captain what are our chances." Miss Browne hurried away.

Marcus and Samantha looked at each other. Samantha twisted a lock of her hair. Marcus reached for her hand. "Hang in there, Sami. Maybe they'll be able to help us."

They stood, hand in hand. Marcus thrust the other

hand deep into the pocket of his trousers.

"Look!" One of the seamen shouted. "There are two tugs coming out. They'll tow us into harbor."

Marcus and Samantha grasped each other's hands tighter. Marcus's fingers caressed the red stone. Maybe they'd make it yet.

Out of nowhere, dizziness struck him. He opened his mouth to say something, looked at Samantha. She had a funny expression on her face.

"Mar-r-r---ko-ooo." Her voice sounded far away. Her body seemed to fade out of his sight.

Marcus swallowed. His breath came short and shallow. He held his sister's hand even tighter. Now he could almost feel waves of...something...wash over him.

Was he ill? What was happening? Blackness crowded around the outer edges of his vision, then faded to nothingness.

CHAPTER 23

"Marcus, Samantha, dinner will be ready in ten minutes. Finish whatever you're doing and come on downstairs."

"Wha...." Marcus shook his head to make the last of the dizziness go away. To his left. Samantha sprawled on the floor. They still held each other's hands.

He pried his hand loose, ran his fingers through his hair. Where were they? He looked around. Home. They were in their playroom upstairs in their very own home. And if the voice he'd heard was the one he thought, his mother was calling which meant they had returned to their own time.

"Sami." He gently shook his sister's shoulder. "Sami, wake up. We're home. Home, Sis. Back in our time, our place."

Samantha opened her eyes, ran her gaze around the room, finally squinted at Marcus. "Marko, did I hear Mom?"

He winced. "You sure did. Dinner's almost ready. Are you okay? Can you get up?"

She frowned. "Of course." Samantha rolled on her side, pushed herself into an upright position. "Whoa. Little bit of dizziness, there." She rubbed her face with her hands. "Marko, what's going on? We were standing on the *Jeanette*, then all of a sudden, I got faint. The next thing I knew, everything started turning black. Then...nada."

"That happened to me, too," said Marcus. "When I woke up, here we were in our playroom with Mom calling us to come to dinner."

Samantha stared at him." So somehow, we got off the *Jeanette* and back to our own place and time. How?"

Marcus shook his head. "I wish I knew."

"Kids, wash up and come on down. We're ready to eat." Their mother's voice demanded their immediate attention.

"Come on, Sami. We probably need to do more than wash our hands." Marcus took a good look at his own clothing and his sister's. "Huh. Funny. We're a bit rumpled, but we don't appear like we've been water-soaked for days."

Samantha conducted her own inspection. "You're right. That's weird."

Marcus pushed her gently toward the door. "Go wash up. I'll meet you downstairs. After we eat we'll come back here and talk. We need some answers."

He followed her across the room. "Oh, Sami?"

"Hmm?"

"Be careful what you say at dinner. We don't want Mom and Dad to think anything's wrong. I'd hate to try to explain where we've been for the past...however long we've been gone."

"Right." Samantha frowned. "Okay. Will do. I'll meet you downstairs."

He pushed past her toward the upstairs bathroom. Clean hands suddenly sounded like a good thing.

# # # #

Five minutes later, hair neatly combed, faces and hands freshly washed, Marcus and Samantha pulled out their chairs at the dining table and seated themselves. Quite a difference from the dining salons of the *Doty* or the *Jeanette*. A twinge of sorrow tugged at his heart. Funny how you could miss people you'd known only a short time. He hoped the crews of the two ships had been rescued. They'd probably wonder where the twins had gone, but maybe they wouldn't remember Marcus and Samantha even being there.

So many questions. So few answers. He clamped his lips together. Great-Uncle Henry would certainly be welcome about now because there was a lot they needed to know. As soon as dinner was over, he and Samantha would have one big powwow. They needed answers...and they needed them fast.

"You kids must really be hungry."

His mother's voice drew Marcus out of his thoughts.

She wrinkled her forehead. "I haven't seen the two of you eat so much in ages. Are you coming down with something?" She reached over and touched Samantha's forehead.

"We're fine, Mom," said Marcus. "You're such a good cook, I can't quit eating."

"You'd better." His mother poked his shoulder. "I made apple cobbler for dessert. Your favorite."

Marcus sighed, pushed his plate away. "Yum. Lead me to it."

Mrs. Willoughby gathered the dinner plates and took them to the kitchen. She returned a few minutes later with a deep dish filled with apple cobbler.

After two bowls, Marcus had to admit he couldn't take another bite. "Great cobbler, Mom. You really are an awesome cook."

Suddenly the face of Miss Frances Browne formed in his mind. A pang of concern struck him.

"Marcus?"

His mother recalled his wandering thoughts. "Are you all right? I declare, you children seem a little strange tonight." She peered at them closely in turn. "You must be trying to get sick."

Marcus took the lead. "We're fine, Mom. We've been…concentrating on a game. Probably tired out our brains."

His father snorted. "Doubtful. But since you've been using so much brain power today, how about putting out a little physical effort and clear the table for your mother."

"Why thank you, dear." Mrs. Willoughby gave her husband a pleased smile. With a twinkle she continued. "And you may have the pleasure of rinsing the dishes and putting them in the dishwasher."

"Busted." Mr. Willoughby's grin made him look like a mischievous boy. He scooted his chair away from the table. "If everybody's finished eating, let's get through with the dishes. There's a TV show coming on I want to watch."

"What are you two going to do?" asked their mother.

"Oh, we'll go upstairs to the playroom."

Mrs. Willoughby frowned. "You've probably played enough games for one day. You need to find another way to spend your time."

"We have to pick up the game we were using," said Marcus. "Then we'll do something else."

In a few minutes the twins finished carrying the dishes into the kitchen and depositing them on the counter for their father to deal with.

Marcus gestured a 'follow me' to Samantha. "We'll be upstairs."

Their parents nodded and resumed joking with each other.

Once in the playroom, Marcus dropped to the floor beside the game board. Samantha resumed her place opposite him.

"What do you think happened?" Samantha's question interrupted Marcus's concentration.

"I wish I knew. Why would we be standing on the deck of the *Jeanette* one minute, and the next find ourselves in our own time and place? And without Mom and Dad knowing we've been somewhere else for several days, not just up here for the afternoon?"

"We need to figure out exactly what's occurred, step by step," said Samantha. "If we compare notes, maybe we can see if our return was caused by something we did, or if it was caused by something beyond our control."

Marcus frowned. "Aren't we Miss Take Charge?"

His sister glared at him. "Marcus, this is serious.

We don't have time to waste arguing. We have to determine how we got here. If it wasn't anything we did…if it was due to some outside force, what's to keep it from sending us back to 1898? Or somewhere else?"

"Good points." Marcus propped his chin on one hand. "Okay. Let's review everything we did before we returned here."

Samantha continued. "Right. We were standing on the deck trying to spot a rescue vessel."

"Yep. One of the seamen saw a steamer headed our way…."

"Miss Frances identified it by name…."

"It wasn't making much headway due to the wind and current being against it." Marcus frowned. "Then somebody spotted two tugboats coming for us."

"No, wait. First, Miss Frances suggested we pray. We were each on one side of her. She held our hands and we prayed."

"Oh, yeah," said Marcus. "I'd forgotten that part. After that was when one of the seamen spotted the two tugboats."

"Yep. Miss Browne decided to go ask the captain about our rescue chances, but we stayed where we were." Excitement colored Samantha's voice. "You and I were still holding hands and a few minutes later…we found ourselves here at home."

"It doesn't make any sense," said Marcus. "We'd held hands once before and nothing happened. There had to be something more."

He sat for a moment, thinking over the earlier events. "Do you remember doing anything else while we stood there, Sami? Any movement you made?"

Samantha sat quiet. She finally shook her head.

"Nope. I didn't do anything. Didn't scratch my head, or rub my tummy…nothing."

"That's it!" Marcus's shout caused Samantha's body to jerk.

"What's it? Have you thought of something, Marko?"

Marcus slid his hand into the pocket of his trousers. A second later, he pulled out his hand and opened his fist. The smooth red stone from the game lay there.

"That's what I did," he said. "I had my hand in my pocket and was rubbing the stone while we stood there holding hands. It has to be the answer, Sami. Somehow a physical connection between us and some part of the game is necessary for the game to work."

Samantha leaned forward. "Like when we got transported to the *Doty*. While we were touching each other, I took the ship token and laid it on one of the Spinning Circles. It must be what sent us back in time and place."

"And then," continued Marcus, "when we were standing on the *Jeanette's* deck, holding hands, with me rubbing the red stone, that brought us back."

"So if we touch, hold a token and put it on a Spinning Circle, it will send us somewhere in space and time." Samantha was triumphant.

"And when we need to come home," Marcus picked up the thread of conversation, "all we have to do is touch, rub the red stone, and we're back."

Pumping a victory fist in the air, Marcus

straightened, and beamed at his sister.

For a moment, Samantha beamed back. But her look faded, and puzzlement took its place.

"What?" Marcus couldn't believe she'd lost her excitement so fast. "What's wrong?"

Samantha studied the board resting on the floor, then fixed her gaze on him. "We're getting too excited too fast, Marko. We have no idea of all the powers the game may have."

"What do you mean?"

"I mean," Samantha said, "there are four other stones besides the red one you had in your pocket. Would they all return us home? Or do different colors do different things? Can they always bring us back or could they take us somewhere we can't get back from? And the tokens with the pictures on them...there are twelve of them that match a picture on the game board. We don't know if they make only a one-time trip somewhere or if we could return, say, to the *Doty* or the *Jeanette*. Or maybe even to some other ship some other time."

Marcus began to see her point. "Hmmm. Yeah, and we don't know what all the portals are for...or the Spinning Circles...or what or where is Deep Underground? You're right, Sami, there's still a lot of important stuff we don't have a clue about."

"So...what are we going to do?" Samantha's voice dropped to a solemn tone she rarely used. "How will we ever know what will happen if we continue to experiment with the game? We might go somewhere...or into some other time...where we can't get back. Or we might wind up in a place even more dangerous than the cargo hold of a ship."

Marcus frowned, pulled at his lower lip. "I guess the question is...do we continue to try to figure out what Great-Uncle Henry invented with the game and how it works...or should we destroy it and prevent it from falling into the wrong hands?"

Samantha's face was equally serious. "I think we need to pray about it, Marcus. I don't want to make a mistake and get into a situation we can't get out of."

"True." Marcus sat for a minute before he reached out and slowly stirred the pile of tokens. "But Sami, look at all these other pictures. Maybe we have a duty to explore the game and see what it can do and where it can take us."

"You just want another adventure, Marcus Willoughby. I know you. Boys. You're all alike."

Marcus pinched her arm with a gentle touch. "And I suppose you don't have any curiosity about where, when, and what the game may take us to?"

"Well-l-l." Samantha was almost able to stop a grin. "I guess I might wonder a little about it."

"I knew you weren't chicken." Marcus gave her an approving pat on the shoulder. "We'll pray, Sami, see what answer we get. Who knows? Maybe there will be somebody in another place or time we can help...I mean, we did try to warn the *Doty* about the bomb."

"But it didn't do any good," said Samantha. "We weren't able to communicate with the *Doty* and tell the captain what was going on."

"No, but we did try. Maybe all we're supposed to do is try to help wherever we wind up." Marcus began to fold the board. "C'mon. Let's put it in the box for the night. We'll study it some more tomorrow and see if we can come up with some other ideas about how it works. I also want to see what kind of pictures are on the other tokens. Maybe we can tell in advance where they might send us."

"Right." Samantha picked up the tokens and stones and poured them into the box. "School's almost out for winter break, so we'll have more time to review the whole situation."

"And maybe," said Marcus, "decide where we want to go on our next adventure."

He stood, caught Samantha's hands in his, pulled her to her feet. "Remember the space on the board right next to the ship picture?"

She nodded. "Oh, yeah. It looked kind of like a jungle."

"Right." Marcus gave her a big smile. "I wonder where that might take us? Or, there was a space ship one...."

THE END

AUTHOR AFTERWORD

When describing events that actually took place, an author often adds details and scenes in a work of fiction that did not actually occur. I have taken the liberty of doing that for the sake of the story in "Eye of the Storm: The First Token."

There was no "Mystery Man" on the *Doty*, nor any bomb. Those were simply created from the author's imagination. However, the other facts of the trip of the *Doty* and the *Olive Jeanette* are as accurate as my research could make them.

The actual cause of the sinking of the *Doty* was never definitely determined. However, when the wreck was finally excavated the location of the ship, and its condition, seemed to indicate that after the towline to the *Jeanette* snapped, the *Doty* probably tried to turn to go help the tow.

Considering the size of the *Doty* and the lack of speed with which it could make such a maneuver, it is highly likely that the vessel was caught in a trough between waves and was swamped in the ferocious storm. It sank to the bottom of Lake Michigan in an upright position with its cargo of corn still intact. The value of the corn, in today's market, would have been worth around one million dollars.

More information regarding the underwater excavation of the site can be found online at: http://www.ship-wreck.com/shipwreck/doty/

A *National Geographic* special was made several years ago and is available for a small fee on YouTube at:
https://www.youtube.com/watch?v=2nq3tE2YETY

D. A. Featherling
October, 2016

Mission to Mars:
The Second Token

—Book 2—
Time Game Series

Join Marcus and Samantha
as they journey to the red planet

Coming — 2017

D. A. Featherling

 # New in 2017

The twins will soon have their very own website! [www.TimeGameSeries.com]. It's not active yet, but check the site after January 1, 2017 for its launch.

There will be new information about the twins, their upcoming adventures, and even Great-Uncle Henry! Plus some videos, bonus stories, and a downloadable fan certificate.

See you soon on the web!

ABOUT THE AUTHOR

D. A. Featherling writes in multiple genres. She has published adult mysteries, romantic comedies, end times fiction, romance, and a book about a non-fiction cold case murder. Her newest project is a time travel adventure series for middle-grade – YA readers.

Her administrative career in corporations, state agencies, and a university physics research center, and as owner of a home staging business, have given her a multitude of ideas and characters for her novels.

She has also written many nonfiction and technical pieces and has won awards for fiction, journalism, and public speaking.

More information is available on her website:
http://www.dafeatherling.com

Books available through author website or
Amazon.com (Soft Cover & Kindle) and
Smashwords (all other e-readers)

BOOKS BY
D. A. FEATHERLING

Mystery

IT'S MURDER AT THE OFFICE SERIES
It Adds Up to Murder (Book 1)
Bubble, Bubble, Toil and…Murder (Book 2)

STAGED FOR MURDER SERIES
Murder Outside the Box (Book 1)
Convention-al Murder (Book 2)

Romantic Comedy/Romance

Sauce for the Goose
Kissing Frogs
Double Trouble
Making Over Caro
Friendly, Michael

End of Times Fiction

OUT OF TIME SERIES
Time Out (Book 1)
Double Time (Book 2)
End of Time (Book 3)

Non-Fiction

Who Killed Ben Miller &
Death of a Juror

Pre-Teen/YA Fiction

Eye of the Storm: The First Token

Made in the USA
Columbia, SC
19 September 2019